Kauai Calling

By
Ron Christmas & Amy King

Pw
Paradise Works, Inc.

Kauai Calling

Copyright © 1998
Library of Congress Catalog Card Number: 98-87531
ISBN: 0-9667110-0-9

Paradise Works, Inc.

First Printing 1998
All rights reserved. No part of this book
may be reproduced in any form, except for the
inclusion of brief quotations in a review or
article, without written permission from the author
or publisher.

Published by: Paradise Works, Inc. P.O. Box 1058
Koloa, Hawaii 96756
(808) 742-2457

Special acknowledgment to Ms. Joy Jobson

This Book is Lovingly Dedicated

to

Becky & David

in Celebration of

Their Wedding Day

April 28th, 2001

&

Honeymoon in Paradise

Maui and Kauai, Hawaii

"The best honeymoon ever!

May our life continue to be one romantic

adventure after another."

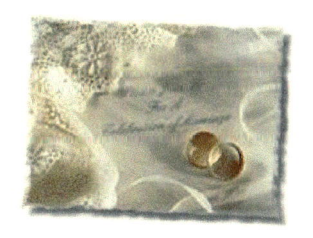

E lei kau, e lei ho'oilo i ke aloha

(Love is Everlasting)

Kauai Calling

Chapter One

At last, Paradise

"Doesn't that air smell heavenly?" Becky said as they stepped out of the waiting room into the open hallway of Lihue Airport. A leafy garden paralleled the walkway and presented weary travelers with a feast for the eyes. She drew in a deep lung full of fresh, warm, moist, tropic air and purred with contentment.

"La Guardia International *never* smelled like this," continued Becky.

"I think you're smelling that Hawaiian woman's leis," David said, pointing to a woman who had a half dozen leis dangling around her neck.

"Oh, they're so beautiful," Becky said. "I wish I had a lei." She and her best friend, Kat, had just been

Kauai Calling

talking this past week about how rare it was these days for a woman to receive flowers, except for those hastily delivered on Valentine's Day when you knew your husband had called the florist to order them and the florist had put together a bouquet of whatever was left in the shop. Did today's men ever go into flower shops on a whim and bring a bouquet of their sweetheart's favorite flowers home as they used too in the old films, they wondered?

Becky smiled at the Hawaiian woman wreathed in flowers. "You are so lucky."

"I love them," the Auntie said in a deep rich voice that promised music. She sniffed each lei in turn, "though they are a wee bit warm to wear when there are so many."

"Would you consider selling one?" David asked.

"Oh, no," the Auntie said, shaking her head vigorously.

"*Honestly*, David, how could you ask that?" Becky whispered.

David shrugged. "Sorry, I *thought* you wanted a lei."

"And you will have one," the Hawaiian woman said, sliding a lush, yellow ginger lei from around her neck. "No one should come to Kauai and not have a lei to greet them."

"How much?" David asked, drawing out his wallet.

"A lei costs only a kiss," the Auntie said. "After

At last, Paradise

you give her the lei, you kiss her."

"Oh, no, please, I couldn't take your beautiful lei," Becky said.

"You cannot, *not* take it," the Auntie answered, emphasizing each word as she handed the yellow ginger lei to David, "it would be rude."

"But your family made it for you," Becky protested.

"That's okay," a young girl from the family said, "we sewed it for her, but she can give it to anyone she pleases and share our aloha."

David slipped the lei over Becky's head and gave her a kiss on the lips. The Auntie and her family clapped.

Becky lifted the fragile blossoms to her nose and took a deep whiff. "Ah, it smells so fragrant," she said. "No perfume could match it. Thank you so very, very much."

"While you are here on Kauai, ask someone to sing you the song that goes with those flowers." the Auntie suggested. "It's called 'My Yellow Ginger Lei' and quite a lovely song. One of my favorites. Aloha, you two. Enjoy your stay on Kauai."

"Aloha," chorused her family members before they turned and walked away.

"See, David, and you said all that aloha stuff was bull and concocted for the tourists."

"I've gotta admit that was quite amazing," David said. He tilted his head, studying her. "You know I like

9

Kauai Calling

the way the yellow of that lei brings out the gold flecks in those brown eyes of yours."

"Well thank you," Becky said, delighting in the unexpected compliment.

They dragged their luggage to curbside. "Whew, you sure brought a lot for one week," David said. "I should have gotten the car first. You stay here with the stuff, while I get it."

"'Sweetie', it looks like other people are just leaving their bags on the curb while they get their cars," Becky said. "Let's pretend we're not at La Guardia International Airport and can be assured that no one will steal them."

"Well, I don't know about that. I'm sure even paradise has your unsavory types." He looked at the other groups of suitcases gathered in clusters on the sidewalk, then shrugged. "Well okay, but not my laptop."

"Oh, God forbid, you should move an inch without your laptop," Becky said. They strolled across the street to the rental counters, amazed that traffic stopped for them. "Remember you promised to only open that thing once a day."

He mumbled, "Mm," as he set the laptop down on the rental counter and freed the latches.

"Beautiful lei," commented the rental car clerk, inhaling. "I love the smell of ginger." After Becky told her their reservation number, she asked, "Would you like an upgrade to a brand-new convertible?"

At last, Paradise

"Ooh," Becky said, her eyes lighting up.

"No," David interrupted, "and please don't even think about trying to sell us insurance either. As far as I'm concerned that's just a rip-off."

Becky's brown eyes clouded and her mouth turned down at the edges. She'd worked really hard to make this trip to Kauai a dream vacation, but it seemed as if David was just along for the ride. She looked at the clerk and shook her head ruefully.

The clerk smiled and said, "It doesn't matter, because today is your lucky day. We are out of sedans, so we'll give you a new convertible at the same rate."

"We'll take it," said Becky.

"See," mumbled David, "they just tried to get us to pay extra."

"Oh David, stop being such a pain in the butt," said Becky, her eyes tearing a little. "And please put that computer away. In the five years we've been together you've never once given yourself wholeheartedly to a vacation. You could at least pretend to be here. Where's your soul? Look around you, even the airport's a garden."

"I'm sorry, you're right," he said, latching the laptop and wrapping his arm around her. "Let's get our convertible and enjoy the day, and I promise to put away the cynicism."

As they rode out of Lihue, they noticed on their right an old mansion set back from the road. In the field out front grazed a donkey and two Clydesdale

11

Kauai Calling

draft horses. A sign on the driveway named it as 'Kilohana' and promised a restaurant and shops.

David surprised Becky by turning into the long driveway, which led up to a sprawling two story manor house with a draft horse and an old fashioned carriage parked out front. The carriage driver, who was wearing a top-hat and tails, saluted them with his riding crop as they walked past. They entered into a wide hall that opened onto an interior garden with a lovely dining lanai. This beautiful open-air restaurant was 'Gaylord's'.

"How about if I treat my favorite lady to our first island meal?"

She hugged him and slipped her arm lovingly around his waist. He gently stroked her shimmering brown hair and pulled her close. Maybe this vacation *would* be just fine, she thought, glad now that she had spoken up at the airport.

The maitre 'd led them to a white, linen-covered table accented with a delicate sprig of colorful orchids, out on the covered terrace which had an expansive view of rolling hills and steep, green mountains in the distance. Flowering vines climbed trellises at each end of the veranda.

"Romantic enough for you?" asked David.

"Perfect," said Becky.

They both enjoyed the charm and reserved elegance of this place. It was if they had truly stepped back in time. Nothing seemed rushed, and their waiter,

At last, Paradise

a young man named Miles, seemed genuine about them having a special moment. Although they had told him nothing about just arriving, could he see "first-time" visitors on their faces? Regardless, David and Becky felt very much at ease.

"Maybe, after lunch we can take a ride in that quaint old horse and buggy."

"Don't push it," he said, running his fingers through his brown hair. "I've already committed myself to a sunset dinner. This coconut-crusted banana cream pie along with all this sweet romance may bring on a diabetic coma."

"Fat chance," she said, but grinned. At least he was trying to flow into the spirit of the vacation.

After they had eatenBecky asked, "Can you imagine what it must have been like to live here in all this luxury back in 1935 when it was built and sugar was king?"

"Yes indeed, pre taxes. In those days you got to keep the money you made. Not like now."

Becky stretched and drew in the sweet smells of the garden. "Could we not talk about money during this vacation?"

"Could you not spend any?" David asked jokingly, his brown eyes twinkling.

On the road to Poipu Becky showed David the map the Hyatt Hotel had sent them. "It says to follow the signs to Poipu, then turn left at the tree tunnel."

13

Kauai Calling

"Do they tell you what a tree tunnel is?" David asked.

As soon as they turned off the highway, the answer became obvious when they spotted two long rows of giant Eucalyptus trees lined up on either side of the road, their branches entwined high over the macadam.

"That m 'dear, is a tree tunnel," Becky said.

They rode down toward the ocean past a reservoir. Mountains etched the horizon on either side. At a T-intersection their road suddenly ended with a stop sign. Across the street little shops, outlined in white lights, crowded the sidewalk.

"The map shows this to be Koloa town. Let's stop," said Becky, "and check out the shops."

"You can go by yourself later. I want a shower." David zipped through the tiny town, then wandered aimlessly up and down the few narrow streets of the town, struggling with the simple directions Becky gave him for the Hyatt Hotel.

When they had come around to the same spot twice, Becky suggested they stop and ask a man who was working in his front yard for help. But David drove right past him.

Becky shook her head. Her friend, Kat, swore men's fear of asking directions came in their DNA with their testosterone. When it came to asking for directions, being obstinate was a trait in men that always seemed to show up.

At last, Paradise

After wandering up and down a few residential streets that seemed to have no correlation to one another or a town plan, they happened on what looked like a new highway. But even that road only continued for a mile or two before it also ended with a stop sign.

"Darndest place I've ever seen for road planning," David grumbled, "Now where do we go?" At that moment Becky spotted the green roofs of the Hyatt Hotel and beyond it a broad sweep of blue ocean. "That way " she instructed.

The circular hotel driveway was bordered by flowers in a myriad of powerful colors and a small reflecting pond. The wide Porte-cochere entrance led into an airy courtyard center that housed tropical birds and winding pathways edged with flowers, then sloped down to a half-moon lanai with a spectacular ocean view. Huge ceramic vases filled with tropical blooms were scattered about the foyer. A genuine feel of old Hawaii was felt immediately. David and Becky were greeted with warm smiles of welcome at the front desk, while their luggage was quickly brought in and their car whisked away.

David looked around, impressed. "It reminds me of a scene from a Fifties movie. Hey, 'Tiny', look at that old ocean liner," he said pointing to a large painting in the lobby. "You really outdid yourself with your choice of accommodations. This is truly beautiful. It has real character, not just flash."

Within minutes they were registered. The front

Kauai Calling

desk clerk welcomed them with a genuinely warm smile, and a beautiful orchid lei.

"I wonder if the service of the hotel can match all of this unnatural beauty?" David casually asked. Before the desk man could reply, a neatly quaffed gentleman with wavy blonde hair and a gentle caring smile, who had been observing from a few feet away, fielded David's question.

"Aloha, my name is Jerry Gibson. I am the general manager here and I can personally assure you that the service will more than meet your highest expectations. Here is my card and if you should have any concerns don't hesitate to contact me."

David, taken aback by the quick and direct response to his thinking out loud thanked the GM and smiled sheepishly.

"That must be the 'Aloha Spirit' that Kat was talking about," David whispered to Becky. At that moment the bellman appeared.

"Here is your bellman, Jimmy, and we hope your stay at the Hyatt Regency Resort and Spa is a memorable one," Mr. Gibson declared.

The bellman stopped at the pool entrance off the lobby and swung open the door to show them the extravagant water park with a series of pools that spilled down the hillside to the beach. Palm trees, cascading waterfalls, circling pathways and Jacuzzi's were placed between the tiered pools flowing downhill. A riot of color from the blooms on the trees and bushes

At last, Paradise

intensified the sapphire blue of the pool water and the turquoise of the sea beyond it.
"Wow!" Becky said.
"Impressive!" David added.
"It's got everything you could possibly want in the way of water activities," Jimmy said. "Over on the far side we even have a giant slide, and up there a pool that looks like a stream and actually travels downhill. Down at the bottom lies a heated saltwater lagoon complete with a sandy beach."
"Amazing," Becky said. "We won't want to leave this place and explore the island."
"Where you folks from?"
"New York, New York" they answered in unison.
"Quite a contrast?"
"Very much so," David answered. "Hey, can you see a sunset from one of your restaurants here?"
"Not this time of year," Jimmy said. "You might want to try the Beach House or Brennecke's. They're both close by and good spots for food and a sunset."
"Does your boss know you recommend the competition?" David asked.
"Sure," he said, as he held the elevator door. "It's all part of the 'Aloha Spirit'. We want you to love our island as much as we do. Brennecke's would be my first choice and it has a view from their dinning room that looks out over the ocean that is just spectacular. It's also a great place to experience the local dining scene. They probably have the island's best selections of

Kauai Calling

freshly caught fish. It's just down the street across from Poipu Beach Park. It's a great way to start your vacation. Make a reservation so you won't be disappointed. Oh, and if you do go, be sure to watch for the green flash."

"What's that?" Becky asked.

"You'll find out," the bellman said. "You see one tonight let me know."

"So do you also recommend a better hotel on Kauai?" David teased.

"That would be impossible," Jimmy answered with a knowing smile.

Brennecke's was located on the second floor of a charming building, which seemed even after 5 PM to be a hub of tourist activity. Across the street was Poipu Beach Park, a relaxing setting with many palm trees and white sandy beaches. David and Becky were no sooner seated at a table open to the ocean, when their waiter, a tall, blonde, young man with a friendly smile, approached and introduced himself as Dan. David and Becky listened intently to Dan's informative recitation of the day's special catch.

"The Ahi slightly charred is my favorite, it's Yellowfin Tuna, another favorite is the Opah a.k.a. Moonfish, it's fairly firm and has a unique sweetness, very ono!" Dan said.

They were unfamiliar with the names of the fish, so decided to follow both of Dan's recommendations,

At last, Paradise

and ordered a bottle of Chardonnay as well.

When Dan returned to serve their wine, he looked out over the horizon and said, "The two of you might get lucky and see a green flash tonight. That horizon looks quite clear."

"What *is* a green flash?" David asked.

Dan shrugged. "I don't really know what it is or why it happens, but when the sky is clear at sunset, no clouds on the horizon, sometimes after the sun sets folks see a green flash where it went down. It's supposed to be lucky."

"Have you ever seen one?" David asked.

"Nope, just like my life. I'm always going in the opposite direction when something great happens."

Becky laughed. "I guess it doesn't happen too often, huh?"

"It's rare," Dan said, "like I said, I've never seen one."

"I sure would like to see it," Becky said.

"Meanwhile living on Kauai isn't exactly hell?" David said.

Dan smiled. "You got that right my friend. We have a phrase that sums it all up 'Lucky we live Kauai'. Well, hope you two see a green flash and if you do, yell for me, will ya? I feel kind of left out never having seen one after being here two years."

"What do you think the green flash comes from?" Becky asked David when their waiter had left.

"Ah, it's probably just a story like that one about

19

Kauai Calling

those little people, what do they call 'em?--the Menehune," said David. "Everyone swears they exist, but nobody sees them. Now what I would like to see instead of some mystical green flash is a whale. Right out there near the surfers."

"And until that whale comes along those surfers don't look too bad either." Becky's brown eyes twinkled.

"Never mind the surfers. You've got me to look at."

"How sweet. You're jealous."

"You wish."

"Boy, give a compliment with one hand and take it back with the other. Really, from a scientific viewpoint what would cause a green flash?"

David shrugged. "If it exists, there's probably some logical explanation. For some reason humans like to romanticize physical phenomena. For instance, take the sunset. We've known for hundreds of years that the sun doesn't really set. The earth turns away from it. Right?"

Becky rolled her eyes and sighed in mock exasperation.

"Wait a minute. Don't go and get all huffy on me," David said. "I'm just explaining the time lag that happens when we romanticize an ordinary, physical happening like a sunset. Take this green flash." He thought for a moment, then continued, "It may be that as the earth turns from the sun, and before it disappears all together, the last rays are seen not through the

At last, Paradise

atmosphere, but through the water. Yellow sun seen through blue water could make a green flash, I suppose."

"David, you're such a romantic!" Becky sarcastically added. "Well, I believe we will see it, if for no other reason than just to convince you to be a little less rational."

"Becky, I hate to break this to you, but I don't want to be a little less rational. I like rationality. It's what makes the world work. What kind of life would we have if the world were run by a bunch of your artsy flakes or new-age type gurus."

"Excuse me, but those artsy and spiritual types bring much needed beauty and wonder into our lives. Can you imagine how dull life would be if we only had businessmen, accountants and tax lawyers?"

"Suit me just fine," he teased.

"I know you think that, but you may also find, 'Sweetie', that 'there is more on heaven and earth than is dreamt of in your philosophy,' just as Horatio was told by Hamlet."

"Hamlet? Now there's a guy one might really want to emulate. Drives his sweetheart mad, causes his mother's death, kills his best friend and gets killed himself. Sorry, Becky, I don't see Hamlet as much of a role model for me."

What a perfect place to take in their first evening in paradise. The ambiance was picturesque and

21

Kauai Calling

romantic. When the sun hovered close to the horizon, David and Becky joined the other diners in the restaurant and those sitting out on the beach in watching for the unique green flash. Just as the sun disappeared behind some low clouds someone in the bar shouted that he saw it, but no one else did. Once the sun was gone, the clouds on the horizon and the others scattered across the sky lit up in fiery tones of red, gold and pink.

David turned his attention back to Becky. "Well, I guess now I don't have to call The New York Times and WNEW to tell them I saw the wondrous green flash of Kauai. Of course, that guy in the bar saw it, but he also sounded as if he'd been toasting the Menehune."

"It doesn't matter," said Becky, drawing in a deep, satisfying breath of sea air. "David, don't those palm trees silhouetted against that crimson sky seem as if they're dancing the hula and the ocean all aflame with the colors of the sky could be a Van Gogh painting. Everything is bathed in a stunning pink."

"Even you, 'Tiny'," David said, lifting his glass of wine to toast her. "I do love you Becky Schamis with every non-romantic bone in my rational, pragmatic body."

"I know," she said, clinking his glass with hers. "I truly know you do and I'm thankful for that. David, I don't want to belabor the point, but romance isn't the right word for what I'm after on this vacation or even what I want from you. If I wanted just romance, I wouldn't have chosen you. Even your old buddy, Jerry, is more romantic. I don't necessarily agree with you, though I do understand what you mean when you say Valentine's Day is a sappy, sentimental holiday promoted by flowers shops and greeting card companies."

"Okay," David said. "So what is it you do want, if it's not romance?"

Becky chewed on her lower lip and stared off to watch the sunset colors on the water intensify, before she looked back at David. After carefully searching his face for a moment, she said, "What I'm hoping will happen to us on Kauai is that our love for one another will grow stronger, that we'll become more as one, that because we're now experiencing something that we both recognize as special at this particular stage of our life together it will help us to learn to enjoy life and each other more." She raised her hand like a traffic cop to stop the question that was forming on his lips. "I know that we now and always have had something special between us, but sometimes with all of the quick pace of today's world we don't give or receive the attention that is so important to everyone; let's rectify that."

A flush of guilt spread over David's features. "I get so caught up in things . . ."

"David, I'm certainly not trying to make you feel bad or change you. I want to enlighten us." Now he looked puzzled. "Let me try to explain. Many of the guidebooks I read said that Kauai was considered the

Kauai Calling

place by all Hawaiians to heal and renew one's spirit. That's why I chose this island over the others. My biggest fear about our relationship is that our individual paths are taking us in different directions. You have your Internet. I have my yoga. I love the arts. You love science. I could give more examples, you and your *beloved* New York Yankees baseball for one, but you get the point. When we first met, we spent so much of our leisure time together, but now . . . Am I making sense to you?"

"Very much so" he said, his brown eyes softening. "I'm not as unaware of the point you are trying to make as you might think. Becky, I would like nothing better than to share a new and special experience with you here on Kauai. Before we left New York I even talked to Jerry about how glad I was that we were coming here because I know how caught up I get in my work, and like the cliche says, 'No one ever wishes they had spent more time at the office on their death bed.' So, Becky, bring it on. I'm ready."

Chapter Two

The Language

David and Becky started their first morning on Kauai having breakfast on their lanai, which overlooked the multi-layered Hyatt Pool. Graceful palm trees swaying against an azure sky and the turquoise blue of the mighty Pacific Ocean served as the perfect background to the rising sun of daybreak.

Becky had to strongly suggest that David not turn on CNN to catch the overnight news and stock report, and he had conceded that the world could probably turn and the stock market could go on without his keeping an eye on them. What actually did get his attention and lured him from the TV was Becky swearing she saw a whale out near the horizon. No TV

Kauai Calling

newscast could compete with David's urge to spot a whale.

While he stared at the ocean through his high-powered binoculars, Becky stopped her ignored recital of the day's plan, leaned back and took a deep breath, all the while delighting in the sunny morning and the eye-filling brilliance of the spectacular panorama before her.

"Sorry, Becky, I'm listening," David said, his eyes still scanning the ocean through the binoculars. "I just don't want to miss that whale, if it surfaces again. You know that ever since I was a little kid I've been fascinated by whales and dolphins. In Pinocchio when all the other little kids screamed as the whale swallowed Geppetto, I cheered and wished it had been me in the belly of that whale."

"'Sweetie', as long as you don't have your nose buried in your laptop or eyes glued to the TV, I'm happy," Becky said. "Look until your heart's content, but listen while I tell you what I thought we might do today. Okay?"

David nodded. Becky smoothed out the map of Kauai on the table.

"First, we'll go to a hula festival at Prince Kuhio Park. It's free and just a few miles away to the west along the south coast. Afterward we could check out Spouting Horn, which according to this map, is only about a mile further along at the end of the road. Let's see, from there we might go up the mountain to see

Waimea Canyon and spend the afternoon in Koke'e State Park. We'll come back here late afternoon, take a swim in the pool, soak in the Jacuzzi, shower, maybe have a picnic supper in Poipu Park and then chalk it up as a full day. I still want to see that green flash. How does that sound?"

"Great, as long as I get to see some whales."

"Hm," she said, "Not too many whales hang out in the mountains. Perhaps we could check out the Maha'ulepu Coast just east of here. I remember the concierge suggested some terrific horseback riding near there. I believe she said it was CJM Country Stables and I'm almost positive that is the name of the stables that Kat had recommended. It would be great fun to experience Kauai on horseback."

"Sounds like a lot to do for one day, especially with jet lag. Before we go any place I have to make two phone calls."

"Business?"

"Yeah," he conceded.

"Then that's it for the day. Right?"

"I promise."

The Maha'ulepu Coast started just beyond Shipwreck Beach, the surfing beach in front of the Hyatt, so they decided to hike it as their morning exercise. As soon as they had ascended the trail to begin their hike, they were immersed in a rugged world of gravelly sandstone, narrow trails lined with delicate wild-flowers and pounding surf that had carved caves

Kauai Calling

out of the sandstone below them. The view before them to the east was as unspoiled, Becky suggested, as it might have been before discovery when only Hawaiians walked along there.

"I don't think so," David said earnestly. "My guess is that a great deal of this sandstone has been washed away over the years. Becky, laughing, took his hand. "David, just pretend, pretend we're Hawaiians living here 300 years ago. Give reality a break for a few moments."

As the two rounded a curve on the cliff, a group of six or seven windsurfers with colorful sails hove into view. "Don't those windsurfers spoil your wilderness picture just a little?" David asked.

"Not at all. Those sails could belong to Polynesians who have just discovered Kauai," Becky said. Before David could respond Becky shouted, "Oh, look! Look! 'Sweetie', a spout!"

That got David's attention. He followed her pointing finger and waited impatiently. Soon a spray of water shot into the air and a sleek, black back, that looked thirty feet long, glittered in the sunlight and arched just slightly above the sea, breaking the surface of the water. As the body of the whale dipped down again its tail came up and slapped the water hard, its divided flukes creating a magnificently huge splash. David hugged Becky, without taking his eyes from the spot.

"Wow," he said, laughing. "I'm glad you brought

us here. It sure would make my vacation to see a whale every morning." Another spout of water shot into the air. "There are two of them!"

They stood transfixed as the two whales spouted, then slapped their flukes in a way that looked as if they were communicating with each other. A booming sound reached David and Becky seconds after each slap.

"Hear that?" David said, almost dancing with excitement. "We're hearing their slaps, but the sound is delayed by the distance. Like when you hear thunder after a lightning flash. Maybe we can figure out how far away they are by how long that boom takes to reach us."

Becky nodded. "I remember you go-one something-two something-three something-and that tells you how close it is."

"One 'something'?" he teased.

"I can't remember the word, but it's two syllables. Sound travels quicker over water, right?"

"No. Sound waves travel at the same rate as always. Water conducts sound better, makes it louder," David said. "The basic reason you hear sound later than you see the events is light travels faster than sound."

"Right. 'Sweetie', you know, sometimes I appreciate that fact loaded brain of yours. Do you think they'll surface again?" she asked.

"Whales usually take a specific amount of time under water between surfacing. If we time how long

29

they're down under water, the next time we probably can predict when they'll resurface. Also from what I've read, fluke slapping in whales is mating display behavior."

"I thought it was pretty sexy," Becky said, batting her eyelashes with exaggeration.

Just then the whales reappeared. First, a slap resounded from one whale, then the next from the other. David started counting the slaps. "Fifteen, 16 . . . . . 21, 22." The whales dove down and David looked at his watch and set the timer. "Last time it took about three minutes. This time I'll get the exact time."

"I'm just so happy we saw them," Becky said. Let's start every morning with a walk along here and greet the whales."

The two whales did reappear almost on schedule every three or four minutes. They watched them intently for close to an hour. David was as excited as a boy in a toy store and seeing him that way warmed Becky's heart. Often when they were together, David seemed distracted by whatever was going on in his head, but at this moment she could feel that every ounce of his being was focused right there.

A thought popped into her head as she watched him and she wondered if she dared mention it to him. It was the kind of idea that usually made him scoff and deride all the flakes and air heads that came up with unscientific nonsense. But this idea had fascinated her since she first heard of it. Even if this wasn't the perfect

The Language

moment to present it to David, she couldn't imagine a better one. She cleared her throat.

"David, I want to ask you about something. I know you may have a little trouble with it, but just hear me out before you dismiss it. Okay?" He looked skeptical already. "Don't give me that look before you even hear what I have to say."

"I can tell by the cautious way you're presenting it that I'm not about to like this idea," he said, his eyes squinting.

Becky waited until he wiped his face clean of skepticism before continuing, "I didn't ask you to believe what I'm about to say, I just asked that you listen."

"Okay, I'm listening," he said, biting back the slight smirk that appeared on his lips.

"Okay. Here goes. I read some place that whales and dolphins are considered psycho-pomps for human beings."

"Psycho-pomps? Is that one word or two?"

"One," she said and quickly went on, "Because they are air breathing mammals living in the sea, they bridge the gap between animals and fish, and therefore are for us symbols of wholeness. That's why we are so entranced with them. On a deep, unconscious, symbolic level we feel that they may have the ability to lead us to our inner or spiritual selves and we also understand that once we incorporate that part of ourselves into our consciousness we become whole."

31

Kauai Calling

David frowned. "Sounds like new-age psycho drivel to me. C'mon, 'Tiny'. Is psycho-pomp really a word? I mean, could it be found in a dictionary, maybe like Webster's, not some new-age flake guide you got from Kat? Confess, Kat told you about psycho-pomps, didn't she?"

"Kat may have mentioned it, but I remember reading about it, too. I can't remember where. But you also could open your mind just a wee bit. Tell me. Why do you think you get so excited when you see a whale? Why have you been drawn to whales and dolphins since you were a little kid?" Becky asked.

David took his eye off the spot in the sea where he'd hoped the whales would reappear. "Because they are magnificent animals and it is their size and unavailability makes them fascinating. Can you imagine Melville writing Moby Dick about a cat. Darn, ten minutes have passed and they still haven't reappeared." He sighed. "Probably that's it for now. Oh well, we'll come back tomorrow. We'd better get on with the day's schedule."

"We can wait a bit longer."

"Nah. That's all right," he said. "We've been here over an hour. I guess I've been psycho-pomped enough for today," he grabbed the hand she swatted him with and, holding it, started back down the path.

"Becky, I'll bet you a box of chocolates Kat made up that word. To me it sounds like a psycho who pumps iron--yeah, my guess is it's made up."

The Language

"Maybe we'll discover the truth during this vacation," Becky said mysteriously.

"Becky, please, don't spoil our vacation with that new-age spiritual mental manure, okay?"

Seeing her face cloud, he pulled her close and said, "Hey, I'm just teasing, sorry for being my stodgy, reality-based self. I really do appreciate your bringing me up here to see the whales. Thank-you for thinking about my wants and needs. Tell you what, the rest of the day I'm yours. In fact every day we see a whale or a dolphin I will be your servant to command."

"Is that a promise?" Becky asked.

"It's a fact."

Back at the hotel they took a quick dip in the pool and even shot down the water slide. David felt only a little foolish when he splashed awkwardly and loudly into the pool below. At one point he could feel his swimming trunks trying to come down, but he didn't care, he knew he was having fun.

After a quick shower and change of clothes they were off once again, this time to see the dance celebration of the hula school, or halau as it is called in Hawaii, at Prince Kuhio Park. When they arrived at the cozy little park with a statue of Hawaiian prince Jonah Kuhio in the center, they found quite a large crowd. With all of the chairs already taken they got comfortable on the grassy lawn.

"The hula dance is part of the Hawaiian religion and not just Hollywood's version of green cellophane

33

Kauai Calling

skirts and hip jiggling," Becky read from the brochure she'd been handed as they entered the park. "It says here for the Kahiko, or old-fashioned kind of Hula, you're not supposed to clap. Watching it and hearing the chants is a celebration of the Hawaiian religion and should be treated with religious solemnity."

David mumbled, "A little bit of hip jiggling might make religion a bit more fun."

Becky shushed him. In a louder voice she read from the flyer, "In the beginning they are going to demonstrate modern hula, the Auwana, which is what happened to the hula when the missionaries came. It says here that the dancers were forced to wear long dresses and the dance itself was made cute and flirty, rather than ceremonial and dramatic."

As they sat waiting the morning sun intensified and David began to sweat. "When is this thing going to start?" he complained, mopping his brow and glancing at his watch. "It's ten minutes late already."

"Hey, brah," a local man sitting next to him said with a grin. "You here on Hawaiian time. Ten minutes, she no late. Early still. Thirty minutes, mm, mebbee on time. One hour, now she gettin' late. It's da kine. Why we no got ulcers."

"Thanks," said David to the man, then whispered to Becky, "What did he say?"

"He said, relax, you're on Hawaiian time. Didn't you notice last night that the local news on TV started five minutes late? Can you imagine that on the

The Language

mainland? I almost changed my watch until I noticed all the clocks in the room agreed with me."

David lay back on the natural carpet of grass, put his hat over his eyes and stretched lazily. The man who had spoken to him smiled and said, "Now you got da kine. Hawaiian time means no rush, enjoy."

At last about 30 minutes late, or just in time, as the local man had suggested, the show began. The younger dancers of the halau, the hula school, performed first. They danced an Auwana number, while a small ensemble of ukelele players sang, "On My Island There Are Rainbows." Next under the watchful eye of their kumu, or teacher, they performed a dance about their tutu, Hawaiian for Grandma. Their last dance was "Beautiful Kauai."

After they finished it, the dancers took the leis from around their necks and holding them in their hands walked down the stone steps and out into the audience sprawled around the grounds on beach chairs and mats. Their Kumu announced that each one of them would select someone in the audience to come on stage and learn to dance with them.

One shy, adorable, little Hawaiian girl, stood in front of David and Becky, but made no move toward them. Soon all the other girls were back on stage with their picks, but this little one just stood there with her head hanging down, paralyzed with shyness.

"Come, Leilani, choose," her kumu urged over the loudspeaker. Her hula sisters called encouragement

35

Kauai Calling

from the stage, "Pick him. That one. Leilani, pick him." Suddenly, David realized what was happening. They wanted her to pick him. "No. No. No," he said, holding up his hand to stop her.

"Hey, brah," the man next to him admonished. "You no can say no to the little wahine. Where's your aloha?"

"David, I'm ashamed of you," whispered Becky, prodding him from behind. "She's a little girl. Help her."

He could not even see the child's face, though he was looking straight at her. Her hair had fallen over it and she had tucked her chin down so far he could only see the top of her head. Her lei dangling in her hand, hung limply by her side.

"Go brah."

"C'mon man."

"David Schamis!" Becky said sharply.

The child's face came up and a pleading, deep brown eye peeked out from between the strands of long dark hair. Two shaking, little hands raised the lei slowly.

The kumu encouraged her progress. "Good Leilani, good girl. Now give him his lei and don't forget his kiss, then bring him up on stage."

David glanced at Becky. Definitely, no help for him there. She looked disgusted. He sought the child's face again. As she lifted her chin, it emerged from the waterfall of her hair. Under her golden skin, her sad face glowed a deep scarlet. Two teary eyes pleaded with him. She stepped forward and awkwardly dropped the lei over his head. Her soft lips brushed his cheek while the sweep of her long hair tickled his nose. The audience and the other dancers on stage cheered loudly. As she held out her hand, she sighed and seemed to relax a little.

But David felt his ordeal was just beginning. He'd always hated to be the center of attention, especially in an activity where he was incompetent. He barely liked being the center of attention when he knew what he was doing unlike his friend Jerry who was truly a ham for attention and would gladly take center stage given the slightest opportunity. But there was no turning back now. He took the tiny hand she offered him and struggled to his feet. As they mounted the steps to the stage, the other hula dancers made a space for them in the center of the first row. Not only was he going to be dancing the hula on stage, he was also going to be front and center. The little dancer faced him with her back to the audience. The music started and the musicians again played, "Beautiful Kauai."

As the music slowly played, the Kumu announced helpful hints over the loudspeaker, but David could not seem to get the hang of it. He swung his hips around wildly as the little girl in front of him shook her head, unsure about how to instruct him. He could see that she wanted him to do something with his knees. She kept pointing at them to show him, but he didn't have a clue as to what it was she wanted. It didn't help a bit that the audience howled each time it happened.

Finally, the kumu suggested one of the older girls help "those two down front."
A stunning, young, Polynesian woman stood before David, smiling. His eyes widened and his mouth gaped. Her beauty literally took his breath away. The audience laughed. His face reddened and he felt as foolish as a boy at his first formal dance.

"Ignore them," the young beauty said, and with her hand she showed him how to bend one knee, then the other so that his hips would swivel naturally. Once he got the hang of the knee movement, she put her hands on his hips and swayed them in time with his knees. The music played along and soon he could do it without help. After the hips, the hands part was easy. When he could move at least somewhat in chorus with the others, David's little teacher came back.

"Sorry," she mumbled, looking very shamed. He felt so bad for her and was determined to forget his embarrassment and do better just for her.

"It's 'cause I have two left feet," he whispered, hoping that taking the blame might help.

"*You do?*" she said, looking down at his feet with astonishment. "I shouldn't have picked you, huh? I sorry. Just you follow me when I do da kine. Okay?"

Somehow they stumbled through it and the audience cheered when he and his little partner went down the steps together. She then took his hand and led him back to Becky and bowed.

"Whew," he said to Becky, "if that was a religious ceremony, somebody is going to burn me at the stake."

"Relax, brah, that kinda hula not serious, just fun," the man next to him said.

But David and Becky didn't stay for the Kahiko Hula because between his embarrassment and the strong glare of the noonday sun David felt it was time to leave. In the break between the two types of hula, he and Becky slipped away.

They drove a mile or two further west to the end of the coast road to find Spouting Horn, where a fissure in the lava rock along the sea made a noisy conch horn sound, then hissed like a steam vent each time a wave erupted through it to send spouts of water twenty to fifty feet into the air. Salt from the spray dried on their faces as they watched. Rubbing it felt like running their fingertips over sandpaper.

David stopped at the booth of a lei seller in the parking-lot and bought Becky a beautiful new ginger lei. "I know you were disappointed," he said, "when the other one turned brown over night."

"In a way I was," she said, "but also intrigued by the energy put into something so ephemeral. The fact that a lei's life is so fleeting, somehow makes it more precious." She looked at the woman in the kiosk, stringing a lei. "This lei must have taken you hours to make."

David interrupted, "Yeah, but not a bad way to make a living, sitting by the sea sewing together flowers

Kauai Calling

while the spouting horn blows."

"But by nightfall that lei will die," she said.

"God, Becky, you sound morbid."

"I don't mean it that way," Becky said. "Actually, I'm fascinated that some leis take longer to make than they can last when they're worn."

"That's right," the woman from behind the counter said, as she threaded her eight inch needle through a group flowers. "Leis are about giving someone a moment of captured beauty."

David stared at the two women, then shrugged. "Must be a woman thing?" he mumbled as the two women smiled at each other.

Later riding up the ever winding Waimea Canyon road, Becky read from their *Paradise Kauai* guide book, "Mark Twain called Waimea Canyon, the Grand Canyon of the Pacific." David pulled off onto a roadside lookout and so they could look back at the panorama of the west side of Kauai below. "Wow," Becky said, "I can't believe we got so high so fast."

The higher they went, the chillier the air grew until both of them were shivering. "Want the top up?" asked David, shivering.

"No. I love this 360 view. Just put the heater on full blast if you're cold."

Up another thousand feet they could see the whole west and southern coasts of the island, as well as the beginning of the canyon. Out in the ocean to their left loomed the ghostly outline of Ni'ihau, the forbidden island, long and flat, a mysterious, shadowy rectangle.

The Language

At the end of Ni'ihau rose a tiny cone of an island, as if standing guard.

"That's Lehua," Becky said, looking at the map.

"I wish we could visit Ni'ihau," David said. "It's supposed to be exactly as it was 100 years ago. I bet there would be no windsurfers to spoil the illusion."

"No can," Becky said. "How do you like my pidgin, 'Sweetie'?"

Farther up the steep, narrow road, they stopped at a dirt pull-off and walked to the unguarded edge to look down into Waimea Canyon. From that spot the canyon side dropped off so quickly and steeply, it seemed as if they were actually hovering over the gorge.

By now the afternoon sun had turned the red dirt of the canyon walls every hue from bright orange to deep crimson to brown umber. Far below them a river snaked along the canyon floor. From their vantage point it seemed unbelievable that such a tiny stream, even with the help of rain could have carved the majestic red walls of the canyon.

"Look, a waterfall," David said, pointing across the canyon. "Can you see it, Becky?"

"Yeah, and isn't that a rainbow coming up from it? Our first Kauai rainbow. I hope we see hundreds of them. The rainbows are what Kat liked best about Kauai. She said she saw them constantly."

"Because it rained all the time."

"She said, they call rain, liquid sunshine here, a blessing, because before you can finish complaining

41

Kauai Calling

about it, it's stopped and you have a glorious rainbow that lasts longer than the shower. Remember the song the hula kids sang about 'on my island there are rainbows'?"

"Too bad we're not a little closer," David said, squinting his eyes in the direction of the waterfall. "I wonder how long it would take to hike down there. It's hard to get a reading on how far away that is or how deep the canyon actually is without a reference point. Something I'd like to do while we're here is swim under a waterfall."

Becky looked straight down the steep, red dirt side of the canyon where they stood. Not even a weed clung to its side. I hope he's not planning a hike down these cliffs, she thought. "Maybe we can find a more accessible one," she said aloud.

Helicopters flew along half way down below them, skirting the walls and startling the wild goats that skittered along the canyon ridges. From that vantage point it looked as if the blades at times were in danger of scraping the canyon walls.

Becky looked at David and thought, This man needs more adventure in his life. Not much of that at the office back in New York. "How about a helicopter ride?" she asked. "That would be a new experience."

"A helicopter ride, huh?" David said, looking at the one below zipping off through the canyon and another skimming the top of a rim. He wasn't sure he liked the idea. "I guess they're safe." Becky didn't seem to notice his hesitancy. "Yeah, let's take a helicopter ride. I'd like to see that waterfall with the rainbow up close.

"I wonder what rainbows look like from helicopters."

"Pretty much as they do on the ground, I think," David said, wondering how he could explain that he didn't really want to fly in a helicopter. "Amazing place, Kauai. Contains a bit of everything that nature has to offer, except snow and ice."

Shortly after the canyon disappeared from view, they entered Kokee State Park. There they lunched at the lodge, and afterwards fed crumbs from their sandwiches to the ever present wild island roosters who strutted freely across the grass and crowed noisily whenever the spirit moved them.

Then they visited the rustic museum next door to the lodge, where they learned quite a bit about the geology and wildlife of Kauai. David took more time than Becky in the museum, because of all the questions that occurred to him as he wandered the exhibit. Inquisitive he was!

Becky stood by the door waiting until she spotted David deep in conversation with the museum curator. Rather than just wait, she went outside to watch and enjoy the hula performance in progress under a great tree.

When David spied her there, he hesitated, nervous about being made to perform again. But he was also intrigued by the dancing, which was much more striking and powerful than what he had seen and

Kauai Calling

participated in that morning. This hula was not just pretty, but it was also potent. The dancers were hunkering down low and stomped their feet in rhythm to a drum pounded by a singer, who chanted in a deep, earthy voice that sent shivers up his spine.

David forgot his fear and walked closer to watch Becky, who sat enthralled and didn't even notice his approach. He took that moment to admire her the way he might if she were a stranger. When she concentrated the way she did now, he thought, she still looked like an innocent child. Sometimes he wished he could respond to new experiences as enthusiastically as she did. It took him longer to be engaged, though he wasn't sure why.

Glancing at the dancers, he noticed that while they moved together, they were not synchronized in a chorus dancing way. Each dancer moved to what she heard and felt rather than worry about keeping in step with her neighbor. With every line of the chant sung by the drummer, a vocal response was made by the dancers. David decided this must be the ancient hula, the Kahiko. It had grandeur and felt religious. When the dancing stopped, no one clapped or moved for a few moments, then everyone took a collective breath and David walked over to Becky. "Pretty powerful stuff, huh?" he said.

"Whew! I could hardly breathe," she answered. "Unforgettable."

They left the lodge area and drove still further up the road to a spot, which overlooked the western, untouched and uncivilized Na pali Coast and the luscious Kalalau Valley. The pictures Kat had taken of this view were the ones they visualized when they thought of Kauai. The view they saw now of the Kalalau Valley fulfilled every fantasy they had of Kauai and then some. The green mountains that encircled the valley had been razored into hundreds of jutting walls by waterfalls and rainfall.

"A mountain with ruffles," joked David. "Impressive."

"The intensity of the colors," said Becky. "Spring green mountains, silvered waterfalls, turquoise sea and orange red canyon. No wonder so many painters live here."

"I think I could live in this valley," David said, peering down.

Becky said, "I read that a leper, who didn't want to be separated from his love, hid down there for years, eluding a sheriff's posse who wanted to isolate him and ship him to Kalaupapa, the leper colony on Molokai Island. He and his wife lived out their days down there. Can you imagine us doing that?"

"Yeah," he said, "with you it might even be fun."

"Well, thank you, David."

A thick mist swept in from the swamp behind them quickly enclosing them in a damp fog. The valley that just moments before entranced them was now lost in silvery gray. Then, from out of the swirl of fog, they heard a strange, guttural voice, chanting.

As the air cleared, they saw off to the side on a

45

Kauai Calling

dirt path, a tall, white haired, old man draped in a cape of orange and red feathers. Clamped on his head was a headdress that also sported similar feathers and swooped up in a swirl. Startled, Becky looked around for someone to ask about the man, but everyone was gone. Apparently they were alone on the mountaintop with only him.

"Listen," said David. "Doesn't that sound like the Hawaiian chanting we heard earlier? Let's go closer. He doesn't even seem to know we're here."

"Do you think he's okay?" Becky asked. "He looks pretty strange to me."

"Now look who is forgetting about the 'Aloha Spirit'," David said, taking her hand and leading her down the slippery, red, loose graveled path to a spot near the old gentleman.

David whispered in Becky's ear, "He reminds me of somebody, somebody I liked. I wish I could remember who it was. Somebody I knew when I was small, I think. Even his chant sounds strangely familiar. God, I'm starting to sound like your zany buddy, Kat."

"Shh, I want to listen," Becky whispered.

The old man's voice vibrated over the valley as if held up by the fog. David felt the prickles raise on the back of his neck.

The old Hawaiian turned suddenly and faced them. He motioned them closer with a gnarled finger. His heavy brow furrowed in a deep scowl as he pointed at David.

"Heyjonahlakdatyonogointhatonewada, he

The Language

said, as he moved his finger from David to the sea.

"Excuse me," David said. "Sorry, I didn't understand you."

"Yonolissen, whooo, beeghouhou," he said, nodding his head for emphasis.

"Like I said, I'm sorry, we're from New York, New York and don't understand the local lingo." But the man ignored him and turned back to his chanting. No amount of urging from David or Becky could get him to glance again in their direction.

"Younolissenbeegwhowho," David said to himself, then to Becky, "C'mon let's go down to the parking-lot and see if someone down there may know what that means."

They walked down the short incline to the parking-lot just as a bright green van full of visitors pulled in. While the tourists unloaded and made their way up the walk, the driver, a short, pudgy fellow with long sideburns leaned against the side of the van and lit a cigarette. David walked over to him and asked him what "Yonolissenbeegwhowho," meant.

"It's pidgin," the van driver said. "Means you better listen to what you've been told or you will be in big trouble." David and Becky took turns describing the strange old man in the feather cape and strange headdress they'd seen up at the lookout. "Sounds like an old Kahuna or some kind of Hawaiian royalty," the driver said. "Those feather capes and head dresses are treasured heirlooms. He still up there?"

"He was when we left," David said.

47

Kauai Calling

"Hey, I'd like to see this guy," the van driver said, "and you had better listen to what he said. Sounds like he's warning you. In Kalalau Valley, whooee, *anything* can happen."

All three of them went up the walk. The mist had cleared and though the lookout railing bulged with excited tourists, where the old man had stood there was no one.

"I swear he was here," David said to the new acquaintance. "A fog rolled in and we suddenly heard chanting in the midst of it. When it cleared a little we saw him. He was right over there. We walked over to listen and he turned, pointed his finger at me and said a bunch of stuff which made no sense. I only remember that last thing I told you."

The driver backed away and raised his palm as if to ward off evil. "Be careful, man. Hawaii is not like where you come from. Spooky stuff happens here. Better do what the old man said or find somebody with bigger magic."

After the driver walked away with his tourists, Becky and David were again alone, still standing on the concrete platform of the lookout, gazing puzzled at the spot where the old Hawaiian had stood. When they turned around to look in all directions for him, they saw another rain cloud blowing in toward them from out of the Alakai Swamp. When it reached them, the cool dampness wet their faces and bodies, then swept out over the valley.

Behind it came a gigantic rainbow, following the

The Language

same path. The rainbow traveled toward them until they were enveloped in the myriad of hues, as one might be captured in the rays of the sun. They saw each other through a vibrant gauze of color.

As a new group of visitors approached the lookout, they pointed at David and Becky and clapped their hands. It was obvious they, too, saw the rainbow surrounding the two of them. David and Becky raised their arms and twirled around in the colors like children. In their delight, they forgot the warning of the old Kahuna.

Heading back down the mountain, David started to explain to Becky about why there was such a high incidence of rainbows in Hawaii.

"'Sweetie'," she said, with a dismissing wave, "put a cork in it. Right now I don't want a scientific explanation of rainbows. Let's just bask in the specialness of the island and then call it a day."

Later that evening they bought some cheese, bread and wine and went to Poipu Park to eat, relax and enjoy the sunset. At the park a gleeful group of locals had gathered. Some were barbecuing, while others sang and played ukeleles and guitars. Mellowness prevailed.

David and Becky gazed at the sinking sun, as they sipped their wine and listened to the variety of music. This sure beat listening to the same old stuff on WNEW back in New York. Between sips Becky held her ginger lei to her nose and purred with contentment. This vacation was turning out even better than her

49

Kauai Calling

fantasy. Any number of times today she'd felt her heart flutter the way it used to when she and David were first in love.

As if reading her mind, David smiled at her, then said, "Just a second. I'll be right back." He walked over to the singing group and asked, "Any of you know "My Yellow Ginger Lei?"

"Oh sure, brah. Everybody knows that tune."

"Could you sing it for my lady," David asked?

"Sure. Be glad to."

"You don't also know any song by Bob Dylan do you?"

"*Sure* we do brah. That man has put out some *classic* tunes over the years." said the husky Hawaiian man who seemed to lead this multi talented musical contingent

"If you could play something, anything, it would make this day complete," said David.

"No problem" the man said.

"Thanks," David sincerely replied.

He was tempted to offer a tip, but decided it might offend the singers. He'd bring over some bread, cheese and wine for their feast instead. Maybe he was getting the hang of this aloha thing.

"Listen to the singers," he said to Becky, as he dropped down beside her. "These next two songs are just for you."

"My Yellow Ginger Lei" was a mellow, Hawaiian ballad just perfect for a sunset on a soft, balmy tropic

The Language

night. The man who sang it had a high sweet tenor, almost a falsetto. David put his arm around Becky, drew her close, and with heads together, they watched the sun slowly set into the sea, while enjoying the different kinds of music. A magical moment indeed!

There was no green flash this night either. But as the sky again turned pink, then deep red, then purple, they lay back on their mats and towels to watch the puffy clouds drift over head. The first bright stars of the evening appeared, and from out of the East a full, orange moon rose over the roof tops of beautiful Poipu.

"Perfect," murmured Becky.

Kauai Calling

Chapter Three

In June

On their second full day Becky and David were up at daybreak and extended their morning walk farther east on the Maha'ulepu coast toward the rising sun. As they walked along, Becky said, "I wonder why we never see sunrises back home."

"Because we're too busy getting ready for the day when it's coming up," David answered. "Besides it's easier to see the sunrise and sunset, or as I would say, 'the earth turning from or toward the sun,' when its happening over water."

"Shame, 'cause I thoroughly enjoy it," Becky said. "I like living with the rhythm of nature, instead of the rhythms created by alarm clocks and indoor lighting.

Kauai Calling

People here seem to get up early . . ."

". . . and go to bed early," David interrupted. "Even the news came on t.v. an hour earlier."

"Well, think about it. Maybe that's why residents of Hawaii have the longest life span in the U.S. They live a more natural lifestyle," Becky said.

"Hmm, I don't know about that," David said. "The indigenous people have a very short life span. It's the Asian heritage people who live longer and they live longer wherever they live. And if they do live longer maybe mainland people, who migrate here, do so because they live at a slower pace and there's less murder, mayhem and traffic deaths. Pretty hard to get yourself killed in a traffic accident if you're going twenty-five miles an hour."

"Do you think you could be happy living here?" Becky asked, turning to watch his expression.

"I don't know. It's a pretty small stage," David answered, brushing a brown curl back from her forehead. "We're used to a much larger arena."

"It would mean leaving our homes and families," Becky's voice sounded a little mournful. "Just imagine life without any gloomy winters. We'd also be ridding ourselves of the rut we're in. At this point in my life a little uncertainty might be invigorating."

"Wouldn't it be great if you could move, and take everything that's important to you with you?" David asked.

"Doesn't sound like much of an adventure,"

In June

Becky answered. "Sounds like you'd be taking your rut with you. If we had to do it over again, I wonder if we would build the same life here as we did in New York?"

"Becky, admit it, our life is pretty good."

"Yeah, but a little too predictable. Not near as much of a challenge as it once was," Becky said. David's gaze was fixed on the horizon. He squatted down, then raised himself up to his toes.

"What are you doing?" Becky asked.

"Becky, did you ever notice that the horizon meets your eye, no matter how tall or short you are?" Puzzled, Becky followed his view plane. A smile spread on her lips as she raised and lowered herself, confirming his discovery. So every horizon is your personal horizon because it meets the level of your gaze. How come I never noticed that before? she wondered. "It kind of confirms what Kat says about each of us inhabiting our own little world."

"Kat's in her own little world, all right," David said. "She would be perfectly at home in the middle ages with all her mystical mumbo jumbo."

Becky gave him a playful punch. "You've gotta admit her life is pretty interesting. Captivating enough to make it into the New York Times two or three times a year."

"Interesting wouldn't be the way I would describe her life. Let's not get on the subject of Kat. Okay? What's on the agenda for today?"

Kauai Calling

Consulting her now dog-eared guidebook, Becky learned that an old cave lay somewhere near by on a stream they had to cross. "Want to see if we can find it?"

"Sure."

When they came to the shallow stream, they saw that they either would have to walk in the water to reach the cave or trudge the muddy path that ran along beside it. David chose the mucky trail, while Becky slogged through the water. Just as David was teasing her about spending the rest of the day sloshing around in her wet sneakers, he slipped on a moss-covered rock and bottomed out in the red mud.

Becky laughed so hard at his awkward descent and the red dirt stain spreading on his new khaki shorts, and she almost fell herself. As soon as he recovered his footing he protested, "If I laughed at you falling on your rear-end like that, you'd call me an insensitive boor."

"I know," she said, still snorting merrily. "You're right. It shouldn't be funny seeing you upended like that, 'Sweetie', but it is. It must be my childish sense of humor."

Around a narrow bend in the stream they found the moss-covered mouth of the cave. The opening hugged the ground and looked like a very tight fit.

"Oh, no. Look, we have to crawl into it," Becky said.

"I'm ready," said David. "Nothing I have on can

In June

be ruined."

"You go and see if it's worth the trip," Becky suggested brightly.

"Aw, Becky, you don't like that icky, dark place," David teased. "You want a Disneyfied paradise, right?"

She answered with an embarrassed smile. Becky had to admit she always enjoyed the romance of a possible exploration more than the grittiness of the actual trip.

David found he could enter the cave without getting on his hands and knees if he squatted down on his haunches and felt his way along. "Are you sure this is an open cave?" he yelled to Becky.

His words struck fear in her that she might be wrong. She hoped it was the right place and not some other opening in the rock wall further down the stream. "David, it says it has a big Banyan tree in the middle. It would have to have light for that, right?"

"You should have brought a flashlight," mumbled David, as he squinted his eyes toward a faint light to his right.

A little further along he found the pathway into the opening. As he walked upright into the cave, the newly risen sun cast its full brilliant light on the red dirt walls of the west side."C'mon, Becky," he yelled. "It's definitely worth it."

Becky looked down at the small entrance and shuddered. She really didn't like tight, dark places. Tight, dark places contained slimy, crawly things that

57

Kauai Calling

slithered on you and stung or bit you. She reminded herself that Hawaii had no snakes, thank God. Not one. But it did have nasty half-foot-long centipedes that stung, gigantic roaches that flew, spiders the size of fists, and those cute but pesky geckos that seemed to always be croaking at night. The thought of encountering any of these critters in the dark made her flesh crawl. Goose bumps the size of hives rose on her arms and legs. How she wished at this moment she were one of those people, like David, who found all earth's denizens fascinating. In their set of friends to be a squeamish woman was verboten.

Becky steeled up her courage and squatted down and duck waddled into the cave. The blackened entry's darkness was deepened by the former brilliance of the sunrise.

David shouted encouragement, "C'mon, 'Tiny', it's worth the apprehension."

She followed the sound of his voice. "Don't stop talking," she said and heard her voice echoing back, shaky and uncertain. She even hated going into a darkened movie theater in the daytime, because it took so long for her eyes to adjust.

"Look to the right," David yelled. "Watch for the light."

When Becky spotted the first dim rays of light, she sighed with relief. Like a latter day Quasimodo she inched along toward it. At last she found an area of the cave that was higher and she could straighten up a

In June

little. Though still hunched over, she was no longer crouched down over her haunches.

"Wow," she heard David say, which spurred her on, until she emerged into a natural round garden enclosed by thirty foot high red walls. From the caves earthen floor grew a number of small trees and one large banyan tree with many roots. Colorful Monarch butterflies by the hundreds fluttered in the air and sipped daintily at a profusion of luminous, orange, tulip-like flowers that shimmered in the sunlight on one of the smaller trees. From the branches of that tree a large bird with a yellow breast trilled a crystal clear melody.

"The Garden of Eden," she whispered, looking around, her mouth open in awe.

"Yep, and without even a snake. Come into my house, madam," he said, like an old time, oily, movie villain, trying to make his brown eyes look diabolic and holding out his hand from a thicket of banyan roots.

She took it and followed him into the root maze. They walked deeper and deeper into the tangled labyrinth. "I feel like Gretel in the fairytale and you're my Hansel," she said, laughing as David pulled her round and round through the thicket until she could barely see out.

"Make sure you drop enough crumbs so we can find our way back," he whispered. He loved exploring new places. Today was his first experience of a banyan tree, though he'd read about them and seen them on

Kauai Calling

Public Television nature shows. But no show could match the majesty of this mighty tree that spread its aerial roots wide across the ground to find enough sustenance and stability to survive in this sandy soil.

"I feel more like Adam, than Hansel," David said. "You know I could be pretty happy living in this place that is so attuned to nature and the earth. Give me a hammock and a shovel and some seeds and I'd recreate the Garden of Eden."

"I think you would miss your laptop and the Internet," Becky scoffed.

"Don't be so sure of that, Ms. Schamis," David said. "Now that I've gone through my withdrawal, I think I could manage pretty nicely without either one."

"Darn, I should have brought a tape recorder to get that one down for posterity."

David smiled wryly. "I'm serious. I could live here. Even though I knew then it was terminally silly, I loved Gilligan's Island when I was a kid. Never missed an episode if I could help it. The magnetic charm of a tropical island permeated even that television foolishness."

Becky swatted him on his muddy butt, then looked at her dirty hand with chagrin and wiped the muck off on a tree branch. At the center of the maze they sat down backs to the main trunk and listened to the birds singing their morning songs.

David broke the spell by reaching for Becky's hand. "We could go native and make love here in our

In June

little bower."

"I don't think so, David," Becky said, withdrawing her hand and shaking herself out of her reverie.

"I thought you wanted to be in the rhythm of nature, go native."

"I don't see any Hawaiians mating in the bushes," she shot back.

"Maybe you haven't been looking under the right bushes."

"No, David. Look, we can stay here all day, pretending we're natives or finish our walk. Believe it or not the most spectacular sights are supposed to be at the end of this coast. The concierge told me there's a bay there where the mother whales give birth to their babies. Let's move on. We've got a lot planned for today."

David studied her for a long moment, then sighed and said, "Okay, I guess logic wins out over desire." He glanced at his watch. "At home we'd be just getting up. One good thing about jet lag, it gets you up with the sun whether you're ready or not."

He held out his hand to pull her to her feet, then led her back out of the maze of banyan tangles. He had known Becky wouldn't go for making love in a public place, but it had been amusing to joke about it.

As David headed toward the cave exit, Becky tugged backward on his hand, resisting for a moment. It was obvious that she didn't want to go back into the

61

blackness after all this beautiful light. He joined her as they both feasted their eyes on the monarch butterflies flitting about the sparkling orange tulip flowers.

He consulted the field guide he had in his pocket. "African Tulip Tree," he said. "That's the name of that tree."

"Perfect name for a spectacular tree in our little Garden of Eden. Are you okay?" she asked, aware that David had reverted to his usual scientific mode.

"Of course," he said. "Why?"

"Well," she answered, almost blushing, "I really want us to have a romantic time here. It's just that I feel uncomfortable . . ."

"I know, 'Tiny'," he said. "It's okay and probably a lot more comfortable to make love in our room."

They scuttled back through the darkened cave, Becky following David. Suddenly, David gasped and stopped. Becky bumped into him, knocking him forward on his knees.

"What? What's the matter?" she whispered, panic rising in her voice. "David!"

"Did you hear that?" he asked, his voice somber.

"What? Hear what?"

"A voice."

"What voice? David, what's going on? C'mon, I want to get out of here."

"You didn't hear somebody, like mumbling . . . like that guy up at the Kalalau Lookout?" David said, adjusting himself back into a squat.

In June

"No. Now can we get out of here first and then talk about it?"

"Okay."

Outside, after she straightened up and gained her composure, Becky studied his face. "What do you think that you heard in there?"

"A kind of muttering, sounded a little like that guy's chanting yesterday. Must have been some kind of aural illusion."

"Hearing things that aren't there is definitely a sign of insanity," Becky teased, relieved that it wasn't something more serious. "Did you see something, too?"

"Aw, never mind. It's probably just jet lag," David said, shivering off his misgiving. "Let's move on; what's next on the agenda?"

"David?" Becky looked at him closely, an unspoken question in her eyes.

"It's nothing, Becky. I've just been spending too much time with you and Kat. Let's go."

Becky knew there was no point in pursuing the issue further. When David clammed up this way, he could not be moved. Still his startled reaction in the cave worried her because it was so unlike him to be spooked that way. She shrugged it off and followed David back up the winding stream to the beach.

After she caught up, she studied him, but he seemed a million miles away. At the beach, they waded out of the stream to the other side and continued eastward along the wet sand. The sun by now had

63

Kauai Calling

risen well above the horizon and a few windsurfers were gliding across the turquoise water, their bright sails glittering. "I wonder how hard that is," David mused, seeming back to his normal self. "It sure looks like fun."

They rounded a bend that revealed a small bay, where the color seemed particularly intense. After they walked around past a spit of sandy beach, they climbed up along an easy trail that skirted the jagged cliffs along the ocean. In some areas the water had carved deep caves beneath the cliff edge so that they actually walked over water. Small bridges of sandstone crossed over other watery pockets.

At the end of the trail, they perched on the edge of a gigantic, black, lava rock that looked over the wide bay. No other person or boat or windsurfer or aircraft was in sight. They leaned their elbows on their knees and stared out across the ocean swells.

C'mon whales. Show yourselves, David thought, repeating that request over and over in his head. Then smiled to himself thinking, Boy, you are beginning to sound like Kat. This place must be getting to me. But despite his derision, he couldn't stop himself from calling the whales.

At last they saw a spout, then another smaller one. "A mother and baby I bet," Becky said, watching the two bodies break the surface of the water. Thank you, David thought, though he wasn't exactly sure

In June

whom he was thanking.

Though they watched for ten minutes more, there were no reappearances of the whales. But it didn't matter, David felt content as he had now enjoyed his daily dose.

After a swim, shower and a wonderful breakfast they headed back up through the always picturesque tree tunnel to the East, or Coconut Coast of the island. As David drove, Becky read about that side of the island from the guidebook. "It says, the Hawaiian kings, before discovery, made the Wailua area on the east side their special province with no commoners allowed."

"Along the northern banks of the Wailua River are a string of heiaus, Hawaiian sacred spots, enclosures of lava stones that create hula platforms, which are used during religious ceremonies," Becky read. "The Wailua River, which snakes below these sites, is the only navigable river in all of Hawaii."

When Becky and David reached the Wailua River they almost laughed. It seemed a bit weird to them to call what at home would be a small creek, a river, but they guessed that if this is the only navigable fresh water you have, you might tend to aggrandize it.

The guide book also had informed them that in the early Hawaiian days, commoners had been forbidden entrance to most of this area, except for the City of Refuge down near the river mouth. Hawaiian justice in those days was harsh and swift for

Kauai Calling

commoners, but anyone who could make it to the City of Refuge area was given sanctuary, no matter what his crime. Not even the kings or Kahuna could touch him.

David wanted to explore the chain of heiaus, to try to understand how it must have been to be a Hawaiian before the intrusion of the West, however, she had made reservations for them to see the famed Fern Grotto. They hoped they could accomplish both their wishes by riding up the river to the Fern Grotto on one of the large tourist barges.

After one look at the barge at the launch site with it's bright colors and commercial look, David swore the Fern Grotto had to be a tourist trap. But the trip only took an hour so he acquiesced with as much grace as he could muster.

On the way up the river, the tour staff, dressed in brown and white Hawaiian costumes, tried to get David up to dance the Hokey-Pokey, but he clung stubbornly to his seat. Becky, gauging his mood, shook her head to the young woman trying to persuade him. David sat glumly while the other tourists danced, disappointed that he could not spot any of the heiaus from the river.

When they reached the Fern Grotto they were herded up concrete walks with guard rails to a wide opening in the mountain, from which dangled thousands of ferns. No one was allowed to enter the cave itself. Instead they were turned outward for a group picture and to listen to the tour guides down below play and sing, "The Hawaiian Wedding Song."

In June

While the singing went on, David rolled his eyes in Becky's direction, but she ignored him. Maybe it was a bit contrived and silly as the Hokey-Pokey, but she loved that song and enjoyed being serenaded.

As they re-boarded the barges, David noticed some kayaks pulling up alongside. "Wish we had gotten here that way instead," he muttered.

One of the boats guides, standing next him, said, "Yeah, more fun. You know, brah, you can take a fork north on this river and get pretty close to Sacred Falls, a waterfall with a pool you can da kine in." Seeing David's puzzled expression, he added. "You can skinny dip, lik dat."

Back at the dock Becky suggested a swim at Lydgate park, but David wanted to either drive up along the river to visit heiaus or rent a kayak and look for the waterfall. "I'd prefer to go to Sacred Falls," he said. The guy on the boat said it's only a short hike from where the north fork of the river ends. We could be up there and back in time for lunch. How about it?" When Becky looked dubious, he added, "Adventure, remember? You could hardly call a taxi trip on that silly barge to a cave with guardrails and a forbidden entrance, an adventure."

He made a good point she had to admit. They rented a kayak, slathered themselves with the mandatory sun screen and launched from the shallow north bank of the river. For a short while they spun in circles in the middle of the river, but eventually they got

67

Kauai Calling

the hang of how to handle the paddles and soon were smoothly scooting along in the water, looking for the north fork. After a few minutes they found it easily and entered a green shrouded gorge that Becky agreed promised more adventure.

After only a fifteen minute journey, they spotted a kayak from the same company pulled up on a rocky shore where the creek narrowed to a shallow stream. Muddy footprints on a thin path enclosed by majestic palm trees led them back through a gorge. Ginger, honeysuckle vines and mountain orchids grew on either side and bathed their path with perfume.

"This is more like it," David said, swatting at a mosquito, the size of a small helicopter.

"I hope we're going the right way David."

"Fresh footprints," David said, pointing to those they were following. "There really isn't any other direction to go in. We're lucky we spotted that other kayak, though I wish no one were around. Then we could skinny-dip. Wouldn't that be cool, swimming au naturel in Hawaii under a waterfall? That guy on the boat said if you time it just right you can be up here alone, because not too many people know about Sacred falls or go there, especially in the morning."

"It's almost noon," Becky said, consulting her watch.

"Yeah, but only one boat. Maybe we'll get lucky."

"I'm not making any promises about skinny dipping until I see what the place looks like and who's

In June

around," Becky said emphatically.

"Now who lacks romance?"

"It's more pride than lack of romance," she said. "Wasn't it Shelley Winters who said, nudity on the stage was disgusting and immoral, but if she were twenty and had a gorgeous body, she'd think it was daring and artistically important?"

"Well, you my dear, have nothing to worry about," David said, patting her bottom, "I like you just the way you are."

"Boy, you sure are frisky today."

David sang in a pleasing baritone, "You do something to me, something that really mystifies me. Tell me, how can it be, you have the power to hypnotize me." He loved all those old torch songs, and was glad they were coming back into vogue.

As they rounded the bend, they met another couple, toweling their wet hair as they walked. "All yours," the man said, as they passed them. "Place was empty when we left and this is the only path."

"Most beautiful spot we've found on the island," the woman said, smiling.

"Guess you get your wish," Becky whispered as they picked their way along. "I hope it's a big waterfall with a cave behind it." They heard the pounding of the water before they saw the spot. David picked up his pace and almost ran. When he rounded the bend, he saw a wide, oval pool at the base of a cascade of water that dropped at least fifty feet. The curved wall from

Kauai Calling

which the broad curtain of water tumbled was shaped like a half moon.

Along the left bank a cleared area in the trees, rocks and leaves provided a place to sit. When they reached it, a small brown hen leading a brood of chicks strutted up to them, an incongruous barnyard sight. This island had chickens practically everywhere, something they never would have expected in Hawaii. From their vantage point on the bank, the falls appeared to have an opening behind it.

"Those man-made Hyatt ones are quite beautiful," David said, "but can't hold a candle to the real thing. Don't think this would be accepted there either," he said, stripping off his swimsuit and without a glance in the direction from which they'd come, plunged in.

"Whoa!" he sputtered when he came up for air. "Is that cold! C'mon, 'Tiny'. It's probably your only opportunity in a lifetime to swim naked in a real waterfall pool. Not too many of these babies back in New York."

"It looks cold," Becky said, holding her hands across her chest to warm herself as if she'd already felt it.

"So what? C'mon, chicken little." He swam toward the cascading falls, while Becky watched with uncertainty from the shore.

She wanted to go in, in fact wanted to swim nude, but had to admit she was pretty uncomfortable.

In June

"What if someone comes?" she yelled. "We could be arrested for indecent exposure."

David laughed. "Becky, I don't think the local gendarmes traipse all the way back here to catch people swimming nude."

Stripped to her swimsuit, Becky stuck a toe in the water and withdrew it as it stung. "Omigod, it's so cold!" Meanwhile David had reached the waterfall and disappeared behind it. She could hear him laughing just faintly over the rumble of the falls. That did it. She glanced back at the path, wishing she could see around the bend, then hurriedly tore off her swimsuit.

She wanted to duck right under as David had done, but could not make herself. With her arms wrapped tightly across her breasts, she tiptoed into the shallow water at the edge. Her features scrunched together in pain.

"No, dive in!" David yelled, as he swam back toward her. "Getting wet that way is torture."

"Don't you dare splash me," she screeched. "I have to get wet my way."

"I won't. I promise. I'm just going to help you." He swam until the water was too shallow, then walked over to her and held out his hand. "It's so fantastic, Becky, you have to do it."

"Okay. Okay. I'm on the way."

"Just get wet all at once," he once again encouraged, taking her hand. "I don't mind the cold now. You'll get used to it easier if you just plunge in."

Kauai Calling

"You plunge, I tiptoe," she said, shivering. "You can't make an apple an orange by asking it to be one."

Taking her hand he gently drew her into the deeper water and soon the bottom dropped off and she sank down in, except for her head, which she held above the water stiffly. "When you get your head wet, it will feel better," he said. He then suddenly pushed his hand down hard on her brown scalp and ducked her under.

"You scoundrel," she said, as she sputtered up again. But he was off swimming toward the waterfall and there was nothing to do but follow him. For a short moment she forgot her nakedness. But when the cold water sluiced across her uncovered breasts and between her legs, she remembered it all too well and swiftly turned to check the path they'd traveled for new arrivals. No one, thank god.

On the far side of the falls they found an indentation which allowed them to slip behind the downpour of water. She watched David disappear, then his hand shot out from through the stream and beckoned her. At first the hard falling water intimidated her, but she soon found the courage to go through it to the recess behind it. They looked out through the silvery screen at a blurry idyllic scene.

"I wish we could have a picture of this moment," David said.

"No way," Becky said, covering her private parts as if a camera were about to go off at any second.

In June

"I'll bet a picture of this moment would warm your heart on some cold, winter night," he said.

"I'll risk the disappointment," she said, laughing. "I wish I had something more than a picture to warm me right now."

After they came out from their hiding place, the pool felt warmer. David turned on his back and floated in it for a few seconds. But Becky, worried that someone might appear, decided now that she'd had the experience she wanted decided she would dry off and get dressed. David kissed her sweetly and let her go.

While Becky dried herself, David dove under the falls to slip back behind the cascading waters one last time, though he didn't know what drew him back. Standing in the space behind it, catching the edge of the hard spray on his palms and splayed fingers, he remembered the voice he'd heard in the cave that morning and wondered what natural phenomenon could have caused it.

What he hadn't told Becky, because he hadn't wanted to face it himself, was that when he had stopped and gasped in the darkness of the cave, he'd also seen an outline in blue, an eerie kind of light of a . . . a what? A skull? Something shaped like a skull? A blue fluorescent outline of a skull? Maybe it was simply some type of ocular illusion created by the change from light to dark. Trying now to focus on that image was like trying to capture a dream, the more intense the conscious focus, the harder it was to see it, but if he

73

Kauai Calling

gave up trying, often it would flash across his mind's eye and be seen peripherally. David now shivered. Interspersed with the falling water he again heard the mysterious guttural chanting. It sounded a warning, or a threat. Even more than the chill of the falling water, that sound made him shiver. What was happening to him on this island? Could he be having a mid-life crisis? Did men his age have mid-life crises? He shook his head as if to dislodge the irrationality that seemed to have suddenly taken up residence.

On shore Becky had her towel wrapped around her like a sarong and with one end was drying her hair. Just as she was about to drop her towel and pull on her swimsuit, she was startled to see four people come round the bend, shouting with delight at their discovery. "David," she hissed. "David, people."

She could not believe the nonchalance with which he waved to the newcomers, and then strolled out of the water as if he were properly clothed. This naked indifference was an aspect of him she was unfamiliar with in their five years together. David always insisted on being properly attired for any event.

While the two couples approached them, Becky stood shivering with her towel wrapped like a tourniquet around her. David grabbed his towel and exclaimed to the newcomers, "It's freezing when you get out, yet well worth it."

"Glad you can swim nude here," a man said. "I didn't even wear a suit." One of the women in the party

In June

was already disrobing. Becky smiled tentatively, then grabbed up her suit and clothes and clutched them with the towel against her chest. Her steps as she walked toward the path were as dainty as a geisha's. David smiled at her care, but did not follow. After he dried off, he put on his swimsuit with the same elan as the others had shown taking off theirs.

Watching David from the path, Becky wanted to swat him for his unabashed staring at one of the two women who had disrobed. Nudity was not something Becky felt comfortable about. Doors in her family's household were always closed and modesty emphasized. A little part of her wished she could be more free of those old constraints. But so what? She'd done it. She couldn't wait to tell Kat.

"Good for you," David said, rounding the bend to kiss her lightly on the cheek. "That took guts and I'm proud of you. Believe me, you'll be glad you did it after you get warm and have time to reflect."

"I'm glad already," she said, deciding not to berate him about his staring. "Thanks for giving me the courage or maybe I should say, the shove."

"That's definitely a highlight of this trip for me," David said. "This is the real Kauai, not the Fern Grotto and dancing the Hokey-Pokey on a tourist barge. Hey, Becky, when are you going to get dressed? That guy said this trail gets a bit more traffic in the afternoon."

Becky looked around for a private place. "I'll hold up my towel," David said, hanging the towel from

75

Kauai Calling

his finger tips and peering over it. Now Becky looked back toward the pool. "Better hurry," he urged, grinning. As she changed, he watched her just as intently as he had watched that other woman and in a way it pleased her, although she put her suit back on in record time.

They next stopped at Lydgate Park, a popular picnic, playground and beach. Very family oriented. The gigantic, lava rock enclosed, ocean pool at Lydgate, was created in the Fifties as a state project. It formed a natural aquarium where people could snorkel and the fish were protected from the larger sea predators.

The ocean proved warm and inviting. They donned their masks and snorkels in the shallows and paddled out into the deeper water to enter a peaceful, turquoise world. Above water, shouts of children filled the air; below, all was silent. Beautifully colored and marked wrasses, angel fish and trumpet fish swam leisurely around them gathering their food, visiting one another and staring back into the goggled faces of the snorkelers.

Becky glanced at David swimming next to her, his body tinted turquoise by the sea. She tapped him on the shoulder and pointed out a large, multicolored fish that looked like a unicorn because of a hornlike protrusion on its snout.

While David searched the crevices in the rocks for hidden species, Becky pursued her unicorn fish. As she watched it, she idly wondered why humans

In June

couldn't live as simply as fish did. Maybe at one time in primitive cultures they did. But now it seemed as if there was never enough time. Was all the scurrying and rushing around in today's world really the correct way to enjoy the preciousness of life? In this tranquil undersea world it suddenly seemed awfully silly.

    A wave splashed over the sea wall and startled David. A moment of panic seized him, though he couldn't imagine why. He'd always been comfortable in the ocean and this little piece of it was even enclosed. He felt a little fearful, almost as if he might drown. This wasn't like him at all. When he raised his head, returning to the world of air and noise, he was much relieved.

    As they sat on their beach towels resting, Becky told David about her thoughts while snorkeling and her disappointment when she lost track of her unicorn fish. Then David surprised himself by revealing to her his fear in the water when a wave washed over the wall and engulfed him.

    Becky tilted her head to the side. "I've noticed you seem more pensive than usual today. I thought maybe it was the jet lag."

    "Maybe. I can't explain it, but ever since we saw that guy that was chanting up in Kokee I've been feeling kind of peculiar, as if something is hovering right behind me ready to pounce." David told her about the face that had startled him in the cave and about hearing the voice again behind the waterfall.

Kauai Calling

Becky looked concerned. "You know, David, Kauai is known as the spiritual place of the islands," Becky said. "The guidebook even cites a few examples of unexplained phenomena that have occurred here. There are stories about Pele appearing as an old woman on the road and awful things happening if you carry a pig across a certain gap in the mountains. Maybe that old Kahuna was a mirage of sorts coming to tell you something. After all, we were the only ones who saw him, and when we did he was enshrouded in mist, though the valley had just been crystal clear. And afterward, where did he go?"

"Becky, you know I don't believe in magic and voodoo type stuff," David said. "People explain natural phenomena they don't understand with ghost stories."

"Then what happened to you this morning in the cave and later behind the waterfall."

"Probably a combination of indigestion and jet lag," he said, dismissing his discomfort with a wave of his hand.

Becky wiggled her eyebrows and said, "Indigestion? That's what Scrooge said and you know what happened to him."

"Enough of this 'X Files' nonsense," David said. "Let's get some lunch."

"I'd like to see the City of Refuge and the playground before we leave. Okay?"

"If you insist."

"You're not afraid you might hear voices in the

In June

heiau, are you?" she teased.

"Wow, I'm so glad I shared those upsetting experiences with you," David said, his voice thick with sarcasm.

"Sorry, David, just teasing. I really do appreciate your telling me. It's kind of strange, but also exciting. Don't you think?"

"Wait until it happens to you, then let me know if it's still exciting."

They walked to the City of Refuge at the far end of the park. Its environs fit the name, a peaceful place of shade and beauty surrounded on two sides by ocean and river. They followed the path through the refuge and tried to imagine the relief a hunted man must have felt on reaching this oasis of peace.

"Any voices?" Becky asked as they emerged back into the open area of the park.

"Nope. Guess it's a refuge from them, too. I'll have to keep that place in mind."

On their walk back they stopped to see the playground, a fascinating place of tunnels and high walkways, unlike any playground either had seen. They were conjecturing about who had designed it when a husky, brown skinned man interjected, "Community people built it. Didn't cost the county a cent. We wanted a place for our keikis to play and we got tired of waiting so we built it ourselves. That's the Hawaiian way. Everybody chipped in to help. Lots of food and music and fun." He looked over at the

Kauai Calling

playground and smiled. "Many a new keiki came from building Kamalani playground."

"It's great," Becky said. "So imaginative."

"Just shows you how government money sometimes messes things up," grumbled David. "Hey, ya' know any good spots for lunch?" he asked the man. "I'm starved."

"Me and my family we got plenty. Join us," the man answered promptly.

"I wasn't hinting for an invitation."

"We wouldn't dream of intruding," Becky added.

"Intruding? You're in Hawaii now. We don't call that intruding. We call it the 'Aloha Spirit'. You hungry, you come eat." Becky and David looked at each other. "Come eat!"

They followed him to a long picnic table which was covered with dishes of unfamiliar looking foods. "These here folks are hungry," the man said to a short lady with long black beautiful hair.

She smiled and said, "Please, sit. Join us. There is so much and it's ono."

The man handed them huge, rectangular, divided paper plates and chopsticks. On the table they saw bite sized raw fish, a brightly colored green seaweed and dish filled with tiny, red squares, the man called lomi lomi salmon. A bowl of what they thought to be purplish brown pudding turned out to be poi. A strange electric appliance held a massive amount of rice that looked as if you could mold it into balls and bounce

In June

it off a wall.

"Wha', you no like local food?" the man asked, then laughed heartily. "No wanna' taste of poi. Hmm, ono."

"It looks delicious," Becky said, not wanting to offend them and the man laughed harder.

"What's this?" She pointed to a bowl containing white pieces of what looked like cartilage hemmed in red.

"Tako poki. Octopus."

While they questioned and he explained, his wife piled their plates high with food. They thanked her profusely, sat down at the table and struggled to eat with the wooden chopsticks. Their host, though friendly, laughed at their awkwardness. The poi reminded Becky of the flour mixture they used for home made tree ornaments when she was a child.

David stared at the raw pieces of fish on his plate, then to avoid insulting his hosts he swallowed them whole, though just the thought of raw fish made him gag. Becky told the couple about their adventures and asked them what they thought about the mysterious Kahuna and the experience David had that morning in the cave and under the waterfall.

"The aina she speak to you," the Hawaiian said.

"The aina?" David asked.

"The land. The aina is the land. Here it is alive, as alive as you are and it speaks to us." Seeing David's puzzlement, the man pointed to his head. "Not here.

Kauai Calling

It's a not voice you hear up here. You hear it here." He then touched his heart. "You better listen, brah. Kauai is speaking to you."

As if to punctuate his comment, the sky opened and a torrent of rain fell down in sheets as dense as a waterfall. They helped their hosts get the remaining food under cover, then thanked them and ran for the car.

"You still want lunch?" Becky asked David, once they were inside.

"Ooh, not right now, unless you can magically produce some delicacies from Peter Luger. God, I hope I don't die tonight after eating that raw fish." he teased.

"What happened to your sense of adventure and trying different things?"

"Their friendliness was extraordinary, but I am not sure if I could get use to the food, but who knows?" Becky replied. The rain beat down on the windshield so hard it seemed as if it might shatter.

"What's next on your agenda, Madam Tour Guide? I hope it's indoors."

"Oh, this won't last," Becky said. "Remember what Kat said, 'By the time you finish complaining about it, the rain is over.' Anyway, our next venture is a helicopter ride, and wait a minute, David," she said, holding up her hands to still his anticipated protest. "I told you Kat said it was the best part of her trip and even Jerry told you to try it."

"I don't think I like helicopters and after that food

In June

I might throw up," he feebly protested.

"Ah, you poor thing, now what happened to *your* spirit of adventure you were pushing on me this morning when I didn't want to make love in a cave or swim nude?"

"You can ride in a helicopter. That doesn't mean I have to go, too."

"Yes, you do. So I have someone to share it with, to point things out to and to ooh and aah with. C'mon I got naked for you."

"What if I get sick?" David asked.

"I'm sure they have air bags."

"I might just as well say yes. No way, they're going to fly in this weather."

"It will stop by the time we get there," Becky said. "Come on. Drive back to the intersection that leads to the airport, near Hilo Hatties to The Will Squyres Helicopter Tours office. The concierge at the hotel told me that they are the only ones he recommends because of their genuine interest in sharing the island. Also, they have a perfect safety record so you can definitely feel safe. Anyway David, it's the only way we can see all of Kauai, it's the best way to see the island. The interior swamp and central mountain Waialeale cannot be experienced any other way." The rain slowed a little, but David still looked dubious. "C'mon, David, please. What's your problem?"

"I just feel uneasy about it," he said, shrugging, then added, "How much does it cost?" he asked.

83

Kauai Calling

"It doesn't matter, besides it's very reasonable and I'm giving it to us as our anniversary gift."

"Only if the rain stops," David said, backing out of the parking stall. He felt pretty confident the rain would serve as a good excuse. It was pouring down.

"Okay. Now you promise if the rain stops you will go on the helicopter tour. Right?" Becky asked.

"Sure."

By the time they reached the Will Squyres office at the Kuhio highway and Ahukini intersection, the rain surprisingly had stopped, just as Becky had predicted. "Probably still raining in the interior. I'm sure they won't take us up," David said, as they walked into quaint waiting area.

"Aloha, I'm Kathy and welcome to Will Squyres."

"You flying today?" he asked the awaiting receptionist.

"Guess what, you're in luck 'cause the storm's disappeared," she said. "Our pilot, Keith, just radioed back that the next people are going to have a spectacular flight. All the waterfalls are pumping. Rainbows are everywhere. Lots of beauty to see today. A little scared?"

"Nah, not really," David said. "I just have a nervous stomach, that doesn't do well even in elevators."

"It will be so beautiful you will forget all about your stomach," Kathy said reassuringly. "I promise."

In June

Becky watched and listened to their interchange with a smug smile. She knew that David's problem wasn't just his stomach. It wasn't often in their life together that she got to be the brave one and she savored the moment.

As they left the Will Squyres office on the short shuttle to the heliport, the sun shone brightly. The helicopter sitting like a giant grasshopper on its pad looked new and spiffy. David reassured himself that these trips happened every day so surely it couldn't be dangerous. The front seat next to the pilot had wrap around glass so one could see through a window below one's feet, too. The pilot introduced himself as Keith and offered a heartfelt welcome to all in their group trying to relieve any apprehensions anyone might have. His manner was very warm and assuring.

The crew fastened earphones over their ears, checked their seatbelts, pointed out the aloha bags, then closed and locked the door, giving a big wave and a friendly smile. They took off straight up, the helicopter rocking gently side to side like a ride at the fair.

David thought, this is okay. I can do this, until they came to the first mountain range just south of Lihue. The copter lurched higher with a sudden jerk as they approached Haupu Mountain.

"Whoops," David said, holding his stomach. Becky took his hand.

"You okay?" asked Keith, through some kind of microphone that played his words through their

Kauai Calling

earphones. "That was an air pocket. We use 'em, like an elevator, to hop over the peaks."

"Great," gulped David.

"That's the Maha'ulepu Coast and the Hyatt down there," Keith said. "See the pool?"

David's queasiness subsided as he stared out the window fascinated. The whole Maha'ulepu Coast stretched out before them. David wished he could spot the cave they had explored that morning. Out in the ocean he thought he saw the outline of a whale. He pointed it out to Becky, just as Keith said, "There's a whale down there. Can you see it, folks?"

From Poipu they traveled inland toward the mountains and soon spotted the gigantic red gorge of Waimea Canyon. A rainbow appeared, but instead of extending the usual half circle this rainbow formed a full 360 degree circle.

"A circle rainbow!" Becky mouthed over the sound of the engines. David could only shake his head. He didn't know such a thing existed, though he'd read that the reason Hawaii had so many rainbows was because the round raindrops here caught the full spectrum of light. But a full circle rainbow? Incredible!

What happens to the pot of gold at the end of this rainbow wondered Becky.

They skirted the canyon walls just as closely as they had seen the other helicopters do when they visited the canyon yesterday by car. Now they could look up and see the tourists lined along the lookouts.

In June

Suddenly they zipped over the winding road and tree tops that defined the perimeter of the canyon and were on their way to the nearby Na Pali Coast. Another full circle rainbow shimmered over the turquoise ocean on one side of the craft, while the glorious panorama of jagged, green, fluted cliffs lined the other.

The helicopter traveled up a deserted green valley past thin slivered mountain walls and hovered near a steep waterfall. Keith pointed out many of the movie locations he had help scout for and told them some of the history of the island. His rendition of a few legends was accompanied by a soothing mix of instrumental music. All around them in shallow gashes in the rock, water fell great distances. David noticed that when he stared at the water cascading past a fixed point, then moved his eyes to the rocky wall next to it, it made it look as if the rocky wall were traveling upward at the same speed as the waterfall.

Must be some kind of optical illusion. He tried to point the phenomenon out to Becky, but couldn't make himself understood with all the engine noise and music.

From the air Kauai looked uninhabited and much more mystical. Most of the island grew wild and untouched beyond the slim perimeter where it looked as if only a few houses clung to the sides of this ocean mountain peak.

The helicopter flew back between mountain ranges into Waialeale Crater. The specially chosen

Kauai Calling

music filled their ears, fitting the majestic moment perfectly. Who could have supposed there would be a time when this type of music would be more appealing for a special time than their Bob Dylan Becky thought.

The top of the crater was enclosed in clouds, which allowed only a thin veneer of sunlight through. As the helicopter circled the walls, waterfalls fell on all sides. They held their breath. Truly the meaning of awe, Becky thought. Awesome. Awe-filled. Both stared, dumbstruck, as the copter seemed to stop in midair to let them experience the mystery and wonderment of Mt. Waialeale.

Finally, they flew out of the crater and the tropical sun once again poured into the helicopter. Becky and David then let out their breath simultaneously.

Becky's smile said, See.

David nodded and mouthed, "You were right."

They skimmed over Wailua Falls where on the Fantasy Island TV show the little dwarf used to yell, "Da plane. Da plane." Becky had wanted to see that beautiful spot, although she found it hard to believe that it had at one time been one of her favorite shows, but her eyes were filled from the crater and she had a hard time absorbing the endless green fields of sugar with the rent in the earth, and those majestic falls.

After the helicopter gently landed, they both were a bit unsteady getting down out of it. The crew

In June

after taking their earphones asked if they had enjoyed their trip and seemed to *genuinely* care. Must be that 'Aloha Spirit' Becky thought.

"Enjoy isn't the word that describes that experience," David said.

"A spiritual communion with the earth," Becky said, nodding her head. "I'm so very glad that we went."

"Me, too," David admitted. "Definitely the best way to see the island."

There was not a thing either of them wanted to do after their ride. "Let's go back to the hotel," David suggested. "Take a soak in the Jacuzzi, a nap, maybe make love and then go to the Hyatt's luau. I think it will take me the rest of the night to absorb what we just saw. It's like that time we went to that art museum and saw so many great paintings so quickly that eyes grew so weary we had to leave before we were through."

"You're right," Becky said. "Same thing."

"And you were right," David added. "Thanks for pushing me. I sure would have hated to miss that ride."

The wonder stayed with them through sweet lovemaking and a cozy nap. They awoke famished and revitalized.

"Let's dress up in the aloha wear we bought and really get festive," Becky said, doing a nude tango across the hotel room.

"Whoa," David chortled. "Didn't take you long to enjoy life sans clothes. Just had to give you the right

89

environment."

"And the right man and the right loving and the right mood," she added. "Tonight I could dance all night."

"Macho men don't dance, "David teased.

"Who wants a macho man," she shot right back?

They had chosen a beautiful evening to experience their first Hawaiian luau, located on the flower-laden grounds of The Hyatt, just off the lobby. It was apparent that others had concurred, as a long line of guests clad in multitudes of colorful aloha apparel had already formed. They were greeted by a lovely Hawaiian girl who carefully placed a gorgeous magenta orchid lei around their necks and directed them over to where the remembrance pictures were being taken with two of the hula dancers against a lush backdrop. Before taking their seats they decided to peruse the offerings from the vendors who were set up to showcase their finely crafted wares. Just as Becky thought she had found the most beautiful Ni'ihau shell lei, she felt herself being tugged away by David.

"Sorry to hurry you Becky, but I really want to get a good seat" David whispered.

Becky and David took their seats and sipped on a Mai Tai and Pina Colada. The entertainment was the perfect accompaniment. The reddened sky colored their cheeks and proclaimed that day was almost gone. Even the winds stilled as day turned to night. All was

In June

calm. All was peace. Life was good.

Soon a bare chested Hawaiian wearing a wrap around malo took the stage and explained the process of cooking the pig. By the time he had finished, the aroma of the freshly baked kalua pork had wafted through the audience making everyone's mouth water in anticipation. A traditional Hawaiian pule or blessing was said and soon each table, a couple at a time was being told that they could go through the buffet line.

"That's the part I'm looking forward to, the feast," said David. And a feast it was and no food ever tasted quite so wonderful.

"The food at Peter Luger was always great but it certainly can't compare to this," David said.

"It's really an unfair comparison, and this ambiance is almost from another world, incredible," replied Becky.

Just as everyone was finishing up dinner and had loaded up on desserts, a collective sound of tribal-like drums came from the stage. Suddenly lights were flashing and the stage was filled with highly charged, ornately dressed, chanting dancers. The show all had eagerly awaited, had begun. At the end of the first two numbers, the band leader, a large gentleman with a big smile, announced "Your host for the evening Gus Lactaoen", a suave and dapper man dressed in white slacks, long-sleeved black shirt and adorned with both a kukui-nut and maile lei.

"Aloha everyone and welcome to the Drums of

91

Kauai Calling

Paradise show," Gus announced.

"**A-lo-ha**" the crowd responded loudly and almost in unison.

"That's music to my ears," Gus said smiling. He then led the crowd in a toast and made everyone repeat 'E loa koa' which meant 'Live long and prosper'. The show continued with many types of dancing and several changes in tempo, ending with a daring performance by a fire dancer. There were many smiles and much applause from the audience as the Polynesian review ended in splendid fashion.

After the luau, David and Becky went for a romantic walk on the beach behind the hotel.

"What a day!" David said, "The cave this morning, the waterfall pool and then that spectacular ride . . . how could we possibly match this day?"

"You'll see," she said, smiling happily. "It's obvious to me that our guide on this vacation is the island itself. Like that Hawaiian said, it's alive and ready to teach us."

"I'm a lucky man to have you in my life Becky Schamis," David said, taking her hand.

Becky looked for the teasing grin and a crack about Kat, but no, he was serious. Wow. We'll have to come to Kauai a bit more often, she thought. He is so much more open and present here.

"You still feeling haunted?" she asked.

"Nah, I think the Mai Tais, the moon and you

In June

cleared that out my mind. I feel absolutely great," David said.

Lying there on the beach, holding hands, they stared at the full moon over the ocean, drifting out on its silver moon-path into the soft, tropical sweetness of the Kauaian night.

Kauai Calling

Chapter Four

Tropical Melodrama

The next morning Becky and David left their hotel early, stopped in Kapaa, on the windward side, for bagels and coffee to go, then headed for a broad beach north of town called Kealia to eat their breakfast. As they spread their towels, they spotted some people in swim suits with rakes and trash bags and asked one of them what was going on.

"This beach is owned by the Hawaiian community," a tall, Hawaiian surfer told them, "and cared for by the guys who surf here. Wanna help? You know you take care of the 'aina, it takes care of you. You know what is the 'aina?"

"Sure," David said. "The land."

"Good. Good," the man said. "The sea and the

Kauai Calling

'aina need our help and they show their appreciation to those who care for them."

"We'd be glad to help," Becky said, getting up.

"Hey, no rush. Finish 'da grinds first," the man said, grinning.

"So how did you guys manage to be in charge of this beautiful beach instead of some hotel?" David asked.

"The sugar company planned to sell it. Everybody protested. Da kine should be for everybody, we said. Best beach on the island. Every group in the community wanted to be in charge. But, we, the surfers, said, 'We surf this beach. We're the ones can make it clean, safe and drug free.' No argument there. We're the only ones that got the muscle to do it. We drew up a contract and everybody signed. Now we gotta put our sweat where our mouth is."

After they finished their coffee and bagels, David and Becky took their plastic bags and picked up trash on the beach. Most of it was debris from boats that washed up from the water. They were surveying the section they'd cleaned with pride when suddenly beyond the lava rock reef wall that stretched out into the ocean a whale breached. After its mighty flop back down on the water, it slapped its flukes again and again as if applauding their efforts.

"See, that whale. He's saying thank you," the Hawaiian surfer said, coming up to them and taking their full trash bags. "You folks is da kine we

Hawaiians want to share our 'aina with. Thanks. Hey, you have one great day." He saluted them and walked off with the bags.

Becky and David were surprised to be relieved so quickly of their duties, but then shrugged. "Glad we're done," David said, "but doing it made me feel more a part of this place."

"How about being applauded by a whale?" Becky asked.

"Well, I don't know if I would go quite that far. I'm sure the whale had something else in mind; like trying to attract a fertile female."

"I'm not so sure," Becky said. "You heard the man. You take care of the 'aina, the 'aina takes care of you. I love that idea and why couldn't it be true."

David shrugged. He didn't want to tell her that he really didn't want to consider a mystical relationship between them and the whale right now, because he'd again heard the chanting of the old Kahuna as he was sprucing up the beach. But even as he dismissed her idea, goose bumps rose on his arms.

Something on this island haunted him. No question about it. The Kahuna's chant had resounded in his brain every day since that first time. As a dream might flash visually to the dreamer during waking hours, the chanting reverberated in his ear. The weirdest part was he couldn't consciously recall the chant at all. If he tried, he'd hear nothing. It only sounded when it chose to sound, giving him no

97

opportunity to examine it with his intellect, in order to discern its meaning.

Above the beach where they had parked their car, they found an old, weed strewn, roadway. A freckled woman surfer dressed in a wetsuit with a few filled trash bags at her feet, stood nearby, studying the surf. They asked her where the narrow road led. She tossed her long red, ponytail behind her back and told them it used to be part of the highway that traveled around the island before the current one was built inland.

"You can walk along it. It follows the ocean and is quite rustic and beautiful. Great place to whale watch and imagine yourself in this place as it used to be. I run here when I can't surf. There are a few breaks in the road where the hurricane and floods washed bridges away, but if you follow the paths you'll see that people have found ways around them."

"A mile or two up that way," she said, pointing, "is Donkey Beach where a lot of folks swim nude, then about five miles after that you'll come to Anahola Beach. Oh and about halfway between Donkey and Anahola Beaches in one of the coves you can see the remnants of a whale that washed up a couple of years ago. Just the ribs are left, but they're massive."

"Shall we?" David asked Becky after the surfer turned back to her study of the waves. "We could get our morning exercise, maybe see that whale carcass and some live whales along the way."

Tropical Melodrama

"Absolutely. It'll be an adventure."

They spotted their applauding whale, or a whale about the same size as they strolled along the crumbling roadside. They kept pace with the whale, and soon were spotting other spouts.

At many spots along the edge the road broke off into red dirt banks that dropped precipitously to the beach or sea. At one place the whole road had given way and dropped into a gorge. They had to travel down to the steep stream bank through a terrain filled with ferns and vines with huge leaves that reminded them of the expensive house plants they cherished back in New York.

As David forded the stream, he heard the chant again and the goose bumps made their appearance along his bare arms once again. It seemed so real that he just had to ask Becky, "You hear anything?"

"No," Becky said. "Why?"

"Aw, nothing. It's just, ah, never mind."

"What, David? You look upset." She rubbed her hand over his arm. "David, are you cold?"

He shook his head. "They're not from cold. I have this eerie feeling. My grandmother used to say, 'Someone just walked over my grave.' That kind of feeling."

Becky laughed. "Really? I'm sorry, David. I don't mean to be laughing at you, but I never thought I'd see the day something upset you this much. Do you suppose his chant was a warning?"

"I don't think I would go quite that far," David scoffed, but he had to admit at least to himself that he definitely felt uneasy.

Becky studied him out of the side of her eyes as they walked along, wondering what exactly was troubling him. But when they came upon a cliff that overlooked Donkey Beach she forgot her concern and was swept away by the spectacular, natural beauty that lay before her. They made their way down the cliff to the beach through vines of purple morning-glories and emerged on a wide strip of sand which ended abruptly in a steep drop to the sea.

Since it was still early, no one had arrived yet on the windswept beach. Huge waves crashed in a shore break that threatened danger and injury. After studying the surf for a few minutes, they decided that neither of them felt quite competent or strong enough to swim there.

David's demur surprised and worried Becky. He rarely passed up inviting water, no matter how rough. Definitely, unlike him. He seemed to have lost his usual confidence. She wondered if he were getting sick. Even his concern about the chanting seemed strange. In her experience, David always dismissed what he couldn't explain scientifically. It had to be quite a strong feeling for him to be so upset and concerned.

After a rest on the beach they decided to venture further north along the old roadway. At every turn they found little secret coves, jutting cliffs, imprints and

Tropical Melodrama

flows in the lava rocks that depicted horses and lions and seals. And not a soul in sight. Just about the time they were feeling they should turn back they came upon the tiny cove with the whale bones the red headed surfer had described. Seeing them, David brightened and seemed to shake off his edginess. He examined them carefully.

"Boy, I would sure love to take this baby back," he said, rubbing his hand along a huge rib bone embedded in the sand.

"I think the airlines might object," Becky said.

David crawled under the still formed rib cage and crouched down in there and thought about how often as a child he'd daydreamed about living in the belly of a whale. In his imagination he put skin on the whale and felt himself bobbing in the deep of the sea. A table, a chair, a bed and a lit candle furnished his cavern. He smiled at the childhood memories he'd created to avoid the demands of his parents. For the first time in a long time he remembered how afraid he'd been as a child that he might fail them, not be smart enough or good enough. In the belly of his whale he had felt safe and okay just as he was. He and his whale would sail around the world and have marvelous adventures.

Then in the middle of his reverie he was startled by the Kahuna's chant. The voice sounded so real to him, he worried he might be hallucinating, which was, as Becky said, a definite sign of insanity. Quickly he scrambled out of his nesting place.

Kauai Calling

Becky turned from watching the waves and said, "I'm hot and tired. Maybe we'd better head back to our car and a safe place to swim."

David slapped his arms and shuddered to shake off this thing that haunted him, then spread out their map on the whale bones. "I think we should go on to Anahola Beach, which is just a little further ahead, take a swim, then get a ride back to our car," he said. "We could call a cab easily, if you'd let me carry my cell phone."

"David, I'd be okay with you bringing the cell phone if you used it only for emergencies and no one from back home called you. But we both know that's not likely. I'm sure we can find a pay phone in town."

A mile or two further along, they came down a cliff that led them onto Anahola Beach, a large semicircle of bay lined with sand and cut in two by a river. They entered at the beach park at the south end.

In a reef enclosed ocean pond they took a refreshing swim. The shallow, warm, water invited Becky to lie on her back and float, while David started his daily laps. Cradled and buoyed by the salty water and unafraid of waves or being carried out to sea, Becky studied the craggy mountain with the outline sometimes called King Kong that loomed up over the bay.

I want to live here the rest of my life, she thought, then wondered at the absoluteness of that statement. Do I want to live here? The rest of my life?

Tropical Melodrama

Could I be happy on an island so far from friends and family? The suddenness of this thought surprised her.

These questions her rational mind raised seemed trivial, almost irrelevant, next to her sudden assurance that this place was home. In her circle she was infamous for always saying she didn't feel at home where she was living. David teased her that if she ever found a place she felt at home in, he would move there with her in a heartbeat. Now she wondered how she would broach the subject of moving to Kauai with him. Despite his promise to move anywhere she felt at home in, she knew change would not come easily.

Why did she even want to move? She kind of knew the answer. The problem with our life right now, she thought, is that all of it seems laid out with no surprises, no new possibilities, except maybe a tragedy, like one of them getting sick, having an accident or dying. Right now, she could see their future and it looked as clear and monotonous as railroad tracks across the plains, a straight line into infinity. No deviation possible from the journey they'd set out on unless some awful tragedy occurred.

Just thinking about it made her shiver. She raised her head and watched David swimming his laps back and forth across the reef enclosed area. She'd never understood how someone could spend an hour every day, swimming back and forth like that, as it looked so boring, though this beautiful ocean cove

Kauai Calling

provided a scenic improvement over the indoor, health club, pool back home. She swam leisurely over to intercept him.

"Hey," he yelped almost crashing into her. "What's going on?"

"I want to talk to you about something."

"Can't it wait until I'm done?"

"How much longer?" she asked.

He glanced at his watch. "Thirty-two minutes."

"No. That's too long."

"Becky, C'mon."

"Can't you just do half of your laps today?"

"You want me to die of a heart attack?"

"For one day's half finished laps?"

"Okay? What?" He rolled his eyes and stood arms akimbo.

"Well, don't get an attitude," Becky said. "I really want to talk to you about something. Right here. In the water."

"It had better be good." She sighed and looked almost as if she might cry. "C'mon, Becky, don't give me that look. Spill it. I want to know what is so important it can't wait a half hour."

"Never mind," Becky said.

"Oh, no. You can't say never mind now. Now that you've interrupted my laps, tell me what's bothering you."

"I just want you to be more receptive to what I say," Becky said, plaintively.

"Becky, I'm listening. Can we cut the Kat routine?"

"Okay. Okay. Just hear me out. While I was staring at that beautiful mountain," she said, pointing at the jagged peaks of Anahola. "I suddenly got this thought." David turned to look at the mountain toward which she was pointing. "I was thinking I would like to live here the rest of my life."

"You what?"

"Wait. Just listen. Our life back in New York seems so cookie cutter boring, the same as everyone else's around us. We're all killing ourselves to get ahead, get more stuff and stuff it in bigger houses. Here it's different. I like going to a beach in the morning and cleaning it. I like getting up at dawn and greeting the day while it's brand new."

"And how do you propose we earn our living here?"

"I don't know, but I'm sure we would find a way. You do almost all your work by computer. The cyber world exists here, too. David, would you just think about it?" She gave him her most disarming smile.

"I'll think about it. But right off the top of my head, my guess is it's a bit romantic to think we can pick up and move to some tropical island and live happily ever after," he said.

"Lots of people here are doing it," Becky said.

"Yeah. But they find it hard to make a living here, too, from what I can see. Neither of us would be

Kauai Calling

happy selling hamburgers at McDonald's."

"David, Carl Jung said that if you listen to your inner voice and pay attention to your dreams and symbols that all the answers for a deeper life will be given to you. Maybe that's the voice you've been hearing, the voice of your inner self wanting you to wake up to a deeper life."

"I haven't heard it mention moving here," David said, but he looked unsure. "Giving some kind of warning about this place, doesn't sound like much of an invitation to me. Becky, are you serious? I mean, when did you get this idea?"

"Just now, staring at that mountain. I was floating on my back and I abruptly seemed to know that in this place I finally would feel at home."

"Oh, no! This is it: home," David said, his voice colored by sarcasm. "Becky, I don't think people decide things this important in that way."

He waded toward shore shaking his head in disbelief. He picked up his towel to dry off, then watched Becky staring up at the mountain as if it were Mecca. Becky seems to be getting as unpredictable as her buddy, Kat, he thought. Why did women always seem to want to change things when they were going well? Actually that wasn't fair. Life with Becky had been pretty easy. Now he was beginning to sound like Jerry, who always complained about the loves in his life. Jerry swore as soon as a man had everything just the way he liked it, his mate at the time would predictably tear it apart.

Out in the water, Becky, ignoring his retreat, stared transfixed at the mountain a while longer. Then reluctantly she pulled her brown eyes away and followed him back to the beach where the outline of Anahola Mountain was hidden by tall Ironwood trees.

As she toweled off, Becky said in a somewhat petulant voice, "I've lived where you wanted to live, followed you, changed jobs when you needed me to. Now I'm asking you to just consider changing your life to fit the life I might want to lead. Why is that so difficult for you?"

"God, why is that so difficult? You want us to pick up and move thousands of miles away on a whim? On a glance at a mountain, a hunk of stone? And you want to know why I have trouble with that? Are you crazy?"

"Don't say that!" Becky yelled. "What I'm proposing is a legitimate consideration for us to think about. I'm going to ask for a sign, like Jung says, to help me know if moving here is something I should do to deepen my life and grow spiritually and if you don't like it, David Schamis, tough."

"Whoa," David said, drawing back as if she had whacked him. "A little touchy, aren't we? So what kind of sign are you looking for? I hope this sign you're after isn't something you can make happen. Becky, honestly, do you realize how crazy all this sounds? It just suddenly occurred to you that we should move here."

Becky let out a sigh. She was being unreasonable. David wasn't the type to turn on a dime. He needed to process everything before he could make decisions. "Well, actually it isn't the first time I thought about it. Yesterday I considered it while I was snorkeling. I was following that unicorn fish. You know unicorns are an important symbol to me."

"Do I know that?" David asked irritably.

"You know I've collected them since I was five," Becky said. "Why else would I do that?"

"My older sister collects Barbie dolls. Are they a symbol for her?" David asked, then laughed and added, "Don't answer that question."

"I won't," Becky said. "Anyway, while I was following that unicorn fish I found myself envying its freedom to go and move as it pleased, not just for two or three weeks once a year, but always until the day it dies."

"You're envying a fish? A fish?"

"Look, if you're just going to laugh at me, I'm not going to talk to you about it. But I want you to know I'm serious." Becky dropped her towel on the sand and walked away from him along the edge of the water.

David stared after her, puzzled. He was about to drop down on their beach mats and read his book when he thought better of it. He could do her the courtesy of considering her ideas. He'd always hated his father's impatience with his mother's dreaminess, sworn he'd never be that kind of man and yet he was a lot like his father.

He threw down his towel and ran on the balls of his feet over the soft sand and quickly caught up with her. "I'm sorry, Becky," he said, feeling bad at the tears he saw in her eyes. "That was ignorant of me. Becky, I'll listen, honest. No attitude, I promise." She said nothing, just looking away.

"You've got to understand you took me by surprise," he continued. "It sounded to me as if you might move, even if I disagreed. It seemed impulsive. In all of our five years together I don't recall you ever reacting quite this spontaneously to an action so monumental."

He knew she was listening, though she still didn't look at him. "You know me, 'David, the old slow moving freight train'. I get going in one direction and can't stop, can't turn and go in another very quickly." Though she didn't look at him, he saw her nod and smile. He had her.

So true, Becky thought. He was like a slow moving freight train coming out of a station, rolling down the track. One might think it was still stopped, but just try standing in front of it and it would mow you down. While she was more like a gazelle jumping back and forth across those tracks ready to rip off in any direction with a second's notice.

"I know it sounds weird, proposing to turn our lives upside down," she said, speaking with conviction. "But, David, something has to change with us. Our

Kauai Calling

lives have become somewhat stale in that we are so predictable."

"I don't get it. What 'something' do you mean?" David asked. "What's wrong with us? We've had a great time here. Last night you were in heaven. What happened?" His brown eyes widened and both hands were turned upward as he stopped in front of her.

"David, nothing happened." Becky sounded exasperated. "We have had a great vacation. Better than I imagined. You've been wonderful. But our life at home seems dull. No dullness is the wrong word. Empty is the word I'm looking for. I want the more that Hamlet speaks of when he tells Horatio that there is more in heaven and earth than is dreamt of in your philosophy."

"Whew, getting pretty esoteric here, aren't we?" David asked. "I'm a simple guy, Becky. I like one and one to add up to two. Horatio wasn't simple. He was a scholar, but he couldn't accept anything as irrational as Hamlet's father's ghost."

"Shakespeare is saying that life consists of more than getting our daily bread and sleepwalking through the day. That's what I'm saying. I don't want our life more complicated. I'd even like it simpler, like the life of that unicorn fish, but I want it to contain depth and mystery. That's what is missing. On this island I can feel the hole in our lives."

David said nothing. He felt confused by her certainty. He rarely thought about philosophical things as Becky did. Like Jerry and most of the men he knew, his career, his work was the central concern of his life. He liked knowing how each day would go, where his life was headed. It gave him a sense of control over the chaos an uncharted course might bring.

They had by now strolled up to where the Anahola River cut into the bay. The water they waded into to cross was much colder than the ocean and ran deeper and more swiftly than they had guessed. David had to take Becky's arm at one point to keep her on her feet, and as he did so, he again heard the chanting voice. Blasted, he thought, what's going on? If it weren't for these cursed voices Becky's proposal probably wouldn't have shaken me so.

On the other side of the river they continued their walk along the beach above the shallow edge of the ocean. At this point on the bay waves traveled in huge rollers into shore and sometimes even crashed onto the beach. One of those large waves had splattered them with brine. Becky felt something heavy thud down on her feet. She looked down and couldn't believe what she saw. A long, iridescent unicorn fish was lying across both her feet.

"It must have been riding on that wave," she said, startled.

"A unicorn fish. Whoa," David whistled. "A sign. A sign."

"It is a sign," she said, squatting down to examine the fish. "It's synchronicity. Exactly, what Jung predicts will happen when one is looking for a sign. It's still alive. We've got to get it back into the water."

Suddenly a large, brown skinned man with curly hair who had been walking toward them when the fish landed, ran up. "What happened?" he asked. "How you catch that Kala?"

"It landed on my feet," Becky said, as David reached for it.

"Careful, man," the Hawaiian said. "Dese Kala have sharp t'orn on 'da tail. See 'em, right dere." He pointed to a rigid sharp projection sticking up between the fish's tail and body.

"Wow," David said, examining it with the tip of his finger, which immediately started to bleed. "That is sharp."

"Yeah, you no wanna mess wi' dem fish," the Hawaiian said. "Tell me again, how ya' catch dis Kala?"

"It just dropped off that big wave. We've got to get it back in the water before it dies."

"Dis fish give itself to you for a reason," the man said. "Why you t'ink?"

Becky said, "Well, I was asking for a sign about perhaps moving here . . . and I remembered following a fish like this one yesterday, which I called a unicorn fish. I told him that I needed some kind of sign if moving here was the right thing to do."

"Whew! And you got it all right. You must be one magical lady. My name is Keala, magic lady," said the handsome Hawaiian man, his white teeth glittering against his brown skin, as he held out his hand. He looked to be in his mid-thirties and had tattooed bracelets circling his upper arms and his wrists and ankles.

They introduced themselves, then Becky watching the fish thrash about asked again, "Can you help us get it back in the water?"

"No, no, that fish, it give itsel' to you. Would you give a gift back to the giver?" the man said.

"What should we do with it?" David asked. "We're staying at a hotel. It would be a shame to just let it lie here and rot. Do you want it for supper?"

"I tell you what," the Hawaiian said. "You come back my place and my wife, she Japanese, she show you how to print a picture of dis here fish, Japanese style. Then if you wan' you can give us your fish for supper."

The man led them back along the beach until they were almost at the north end, far from the beach park. Lorna, his wife, a tiny woman, one quarter his size with almond-shaped eyes, small features and straight midnight dark hair, greeted them warmly. After her husband explained about the fish, Lorna pulled out jars of what looked like kindergarten paints and a large roll of rice paper and placed all of it on the kitchen table.

"We will paint the fish with the color you choose and then press it on this rice paper," she said. "It's called Gyotaku painting. It's the way the Japanese fishermen could keep score on the special fish they caught. They'd press them in paint, make a print, then eat them. That way they could brag to their friends and follow it up with proof."

Becky and David chose a bright green color for their fish, since that was its predominant hue, although nothing man-made could capture the beautiful iridescence of its scales. They smeared the now dead fish with the green paint, then carefully lifted it and pressed it down on the rice paper.

But the three times they did it, the print was smeared. The skill of successful Gyotaku printing was beyond them, though at first they thought the task of slathering a fish with paint and flopping it down on rice paper would be as simple as finger-painting in kindergarten. After the third try, Lorna took charge and pressed the fish all at once, producing a perfect shimmery, green print of the fish, which included even its fins.

Then she swiftly painted in the details that were missing, a red mouth, a silvery thorn and a glinting yellow eye. To finish it up she produced an old wooden stamp with Japanese lettering on it. After wetting it on a red stamp pad, she pressed it down on the side of the paper.

"That makes it official," she said. "It is my family's stamp. My father would frame these prints and hang them on his walls in our old plantation house. You can see one of them over there." She pointed to a long narrow print of a great fish.

"It's really quite beautiful," Becky said, studying it. "A work of art. Thank you so much."

Keala offered them a cool drink and invited them to stay for lunch. They accepted the drink but refused lunch, since they were anxious to get back to their car.

"Could we use your phone? We need a ride to Kealia Beach where we left our car," David said.

"Hey, you no need to get one cab. I give you ride. But I take you one special place first. Place, no tourist get to see, 'da Slippery slide. You like it I know."

"No, Keala," Lorna said. "Too dangerous today. Look at those clouds over the mountain."

Becky and David checked the weather outside over the mountain, then followed the ensuing argument between the couple as if it were a ping-pong game.

"I show them, they no like, they no go!" Keala shouted, ending the discussion.

They thanked Lorna again for giving them the fish print and insisted she keep the fish for supper, then followed Keala out to his small, old, rusty truck parked in the front yard. It looked like it had sat in that spot for years rusting, the original color of the paint barely discernable. Becky peered inside at the ripped upholstery and a huge accumulation of trash, wondering how the two of them even could fit in there.

"Not in dere," Keala said, laughing and dropping the tailgate with a thud. "Sit back here and buckle up. Where we goin' you could bounce out."

They snapped the buckles on the seatbelts that

dangled from an old truck bench under the window of the cab. They faced backward as they traveled south on the highway. Their relief was palpable when they spotted the first view of Kealia Beach. But instead of turning in at the entrance to the beach where they could see their car, Keala turned toward the mountains and traveled back a bumpy road that got bumpier the further along they went. Soon there was no pavement, just stalks of bright green sugar cane, red dirt and a muddy trail filled with deep ruts and potholes.

"God, where is he taking us?" Becky shouted over the ineffective, noisy muffler. Her teeth clattered loudly with each jolt as she tried to speak. David clung to the side of the truck and held his arm tightly around her. He let go for a moment to bang on the truck window. He mimed a plea to Keala to stop, but Keala only laughed.

"Wherever it is, I think we're going whether we want to or not," David said.

"My butt is sore," Becky complained.

"This Slippery Slide place better be good," David answered, feeling very inadequate at his inability to stop this maniac from roaring down this trail in a truck that looked and sounded as if it would fall apart any second.

"What if he is going to rob us and leave us back here to rot?" Becky asked as they bounced along the deserted trail. "It doesn't look like anybody has been over this road for years. David, knock on that window

again see if you can get him to stop before I throw up."
    David banged and banged, but this time Keala didn't even turn around. The only answer he gave was a wave of dismissal. David didn't want to let on to Becky that he was a little worried, too. He wondered if maybe Keala's wife had been so adamant about their not going because she suspected he was up to no good. She'd kept saying it was too dangerous. Dangerous in what way, he wondered now.
    Could he even bring down such a big guy if he had to? He didn't like the feeling that he had no clue as to how to gain back control of this situation. It was his job to protect Becky and right now he couldn't. The island and its people at this moment felt strange and unfathomable to him. Move here? Not likely.
    At a strange, stone monument in the middle of the road Keala suddenly veered left on the trail and crashed through a field of elephant grass and sparse sugar cane. Both Becky and David held on for dear life. It was impossible to even talk to each other.
    At an old barbed wire fence Keala jammed on the brakes, and when the truck lurched to a stop, jumped out. He slammed his truck door shut, but it fell back open and hung askew, looking as forlorn and useless as David felt.
    "How you folks?" Keala asked, laughing as he rounded the truck. "A little shook up? 'Dem shocks been dead for a long time."
    "We noticed," David said. "Look, we had no idea

we'd be coming back into such a barren area. I'm not sure we want to take the time to go any further."

"Ah, dat's what you t'ink now. When you get a ride down that slide, you be glad. Come on, 'dis way." In seconds Keala was under the barb wire and flip-flopping down the trail.

"We might as well follow him," David said to Becky. "We're not going any place without him."

"He left his keys in the ignition," Becky said, peering in the truck window.

"You want me to steal his truck?" David asked, his voice rising with incredulity. "I don't think so. C'mon, you wanted adventure. Well, you got it, Ms. Schamis."

The path they followed behind Keala twisted and turned with what seemed no logic or reason. A profusion of tropical flowers perfumed their pathway. Becky had thought the huge, beautiful blossoms at the Hyatt were cultivated tropical flowers, but here crab claws, torch ginger, yellow ginger, spider lilies, heliconia, even orchids grew wild and were just as lush. The trail itself was dusty and soon their mouths were dry from thirst, as well as fear. Like any path into the unknown it seemed long, because they had no idea where or when it would end.

Keala crashed on ahead, not waiting for them or talking to them. Even if they had wanted to, they were not sure they could find their way back after the first five minutes.

Tropical Melodrama

"David, I hope you are feeling okay about this adventure, because I'm really scared," Becky said. "I don't like this."

"I'm fine, 'Tiny'," he said in a voice that he hoped sounded more confident than he felt. "I'm sure we'll be fine. I think the guy is trustworthy if a little over enthusiastic."

"Here it 'tis. One slippery slide!" shouted Keala finally.

Coming off the trail they saw a half moon lava tube about ten feet long, which lay on a deep slant in the center of a stream of water. Water spilled down over the bottom of it in a shallow stream, like a flume ride down a hollowed out kiddies' sliding board. At the bottom the lava tube dropped into a deep, dark pool of swirling water.

"You wan' I should go first?" Keala asked, laughing, as excited as a little kid.

"I guess," David said, puzzled. "How come this is supposed to be so dangerous? Doesn't look very scary."

"You see that one pool down dere at the bottom?" Keala asked.

They looked at the almost black pool and nodded.

"No go down into it or you might not come up again." Keala nodded his head up and down.

"A whirlpool?" David asked.

Keala shrugged. "I don' know if it's da kine, but

119

it's bad. Also you gotta watch da mountains. Big rain show up here quick and carry you away down stream."

Keala stepped out of his slippers, held onto the side of the lava rock tube and watched the water, waited . . . and watched.

"What are you waiting for?" Becky asked.

"To make sure I go down dere right," Keala said. "Don't get caught in the bottom water."

In an instant he popped his large frame over the edge of the tube and shot down it to the pool below. He flattened out his body and he hit the water and quickly popped up above the pool and swam to the edge and climbed out."

"Go ahead, brah, you try," he said to David.

David looked a little dubious. "You need to make sure you go down at a certain speed so it doesn't drag you under?" he asked.

"Yeah, I tell you when," Keala said.

"David, I don't think . . ." Becky said

"C'mon, man, it's fun," Keala interrupted. "You ain't gonna to let some woman scare ya?"

A little uncertain David grabbed the sides of the tube as Keala had and made ready to jump.

"David?" He glanced back at her. Becky looked upset.

"Go, brah," Keala yelled and in an instant David was over the side and sliding down the tube on the cold water. The slide water shot him into the pool and he felt himself pulled down into the icy blackness.

Tropical Melodrama

Suddenly the Kahuna's chant drummed inside his ears. For an instant panic grabbed him. Then he scrambled to fight free of the maelstrom. Becky was screaming his name as he surfaced.

"No go so deep, next time," Keala said. "Hey, you, Becky, wanna go."

Becky looked at David. "It's a little scary in the pool," he said. "It feels as if it's pulling you down."

"You just gotta go da right way," Keala said, poising himself over the tube again to show them. "You watch da water and when it's right, you go." These last words flew out of his mouth as he jumped over the edge and tore down the tube on a fast flow. At the bottom he flattened out his huge body and slid across the top avoiding going under water. "Try, lik dat," he said, climbing out smiling.

David wanted to do it again, now that he thought he understood the necessity for caution. The next time he didn't go under so far even though Keala came down almost on top of him. The third time he really had the hang of it and thoroughly enjoyed it. He was ready to go a fourth time when Keala, scanning the sky over the central mountain said, "It's raining back 'dere. We gotta go soon."

"Just one more time," David said. In an instant he was over the side and flying down the tube. Keala shrugged and went down right after him.

Keala clapped David on the back, as they both reached the bank. "Now you true Hawaiian. 'Dis was

121

Kauai Calling

our fun back in little kid time." David beamed at the compliment.

Becky was still reluctant, but hated being left out. She stared at the black, smooth slide, then studied the pool that swirled in a circle like a bathtub draining.

"C'mon Becky, you're the one craving adventure," David said. "Give it a whirl. No pun intended. Just don't go down straight in feet first. Flatten out, like you're doing a flat out cannon ball."

Becky held the sides of the tube cautiously. She had no intention of just jumping in. If she was going to go down this thing it would be slowly, under control. Keala must have yelled five times before she slipped over the side into the tube. She held onto the edges as her body fought with gravity to get free. But finally gravity won and tore her loose. At the bottom of the slide she slipped into the water feet first and went straight down into the whirlpool.

Big raindrops fell on David and Keala as they quickly searched the water for Becky's reappearance. Before Keala could warn him about the danger from the rain, David was shooting down the tube again, this time head first. The heavier water flow and momentum sent him flying down to dive deep into the whirlpool and find Becky.

Once in the pool he let himself be dragged down. He held his breath and groped for Becky. He could see nothing in the churning black water. When he was out of breath he fought to rise out of the clutches of the

Tropical Melodrama

whirlpool. Keala came ripping down on top of him. His entry into the water popped David up out of danger.

When Keala reached the bank he shouted to him, pointed down stream and ran in that direction. David struggled out of the circling current, swam to shore and followed Keala. David saw a flash of red in the water below and he prayed Keala was right and it was Becky. Keala tore through the bush after her.

David followed close behind. The sharp rocks cut David's feet, but did not slow him down. Giant Hau, bush like trees with huge broad leaves, blocked him at every turn, but he scrambled over and under them with total abandon until he was almost abreast of Keala.

A sudden surge of water brought the stream over its bank and at his feet. The rain now drove down on David's head, blinding him. His knees banged on rocks, his elbows scraped sharp lava.

He saw Becky grab a limb of one of the hau bushes lying over the stream. For an instant, she held fast, her body pulling at her arms. But the water wanted her back. David's breath seemed to be tearing from his lungs as he lunged after her.

Just as he came to the tree she held onto, a surge of water ripped her hands free and she sped down stream again. Keala tore into the rushing, fast-rising water and with the ungainly grace of a brown bear dived down after her.

Kauai Calling

Keala grabbed her foot and swimsuit at the same time in his huge hands. Her limp body swung around banging into the rocks. For a long moment it seemed as if Keala could not hold her against the rushing torrent, but soon he had her up in his broad arms. David stumbled toward them as Keala carried her from the rushing stream to the bank. David's heart thumped in his chest. He still didn't know if she were alive or dead.

Keala rolled her down on a clear spot and turned her over on her stomach, her head to the side. He then pressed on her back and water dribbled from her mouth. When he reached her, David quickly rolled her over on her back and tried to remember the CPR he'd been taught. He held her nose with his fingers, clamped his mouth over hers and started breathing for her. He swore in that moment if God would let her live he would spend the rest of his life on Kauai or wherever she wanted.

She coughed and a mouthful of water bubbled up from her chest. He turned her over so she could spit out what water was still left in her lungs.

"Whew, 'dat was a close one, brah," Keala said, still breathless.

David couldn't stop the tears that swept down his face. He swiped at them, realizing he hadn't cried since he was a child. Grabbing Becky up in his arms as soon as she regained consciousness, he held her tightly and rocked her back and forth, more to comfort himself, than her.

At first, she clung to him, occasionally spilling more water down his back. But he held her so tightly it was hard for her to breathe, she finally had to ask him to let her go.

"Sorry, brah," Keala said, over and over. "My missus is right, too dangerous. Glad you okay, sistah."

"Hey, man, don't be sorry," David said. "You risked your life getting her out. I couldn't do it. If you hadn't been here . . ."

Becky looked down at her suit askew and half off and realized at this moment modesty meant nothing to her. She was just so grateful to be alive. The cuts that bled and bruises that rose and turned color as she sat there didn't even hurt.

All three of them bore wounds from the rescue. Keala had a huge gash in his leg and the skin was gone from one of his palms. David's feet were bleeding and bruised. Using the branches of the Hau bush they pulled themselves upright and tried to find a painless way to walk back.

"How will we get back to the truck?" David asked.

"Aw, 'dis is nuthin'," Keala scoffed. "You should see me afta' one pig hunt. If you can make it, brah, I can carry her. She ain't nothin' compared to hauling a pig carcass down a mountain side."

Keala's struggle in lifting Becky belied his bragging about his abilities. Watching him, David felt grateful and at the same time annoyed. He hated seeing

Kauai Calling

Keala carrying his lady. But he knew he could never make it back to the truck with her. He could barely manage to drag himself through the bush.

Not a word was spoken on the long trudge back. Keala and David had all they could do to stay upright. David barely glanced at the Slippery Slide as they passed it. By now the water in the trough was so high it spilled over the edges. The pool below showed a wide circling drain into the endless bottom. If had gone down just a few moments later, he thought, probably all of them would have died.

Becky cradled in Keala's strong arms, at first startled nervously each time he stumbled or lost his footing, but after a while she found she enjoyed the ride, like when her father carried her as a child. She felt safe and treasured. It hardly fit the picture she had of herself as a strong, independent woman and surprised her that she could be so enthralled by Keala's caveman strength. She glanced at David following behind, he would be shocked if he knew.

She laid her head on Keala's shoulder and thought of Tarzan and Jane in the jungle. His step had grown steadier and more assured as they went along. She let go to the rhythm of it and the ease she felt in his arms. Becky and Keala of Kauai. She sighed wondering how Jerry, David's buddy, might respond to her new insight into her primitive longings. Jerry insisted that what modern women really wanted was a caveman, which was why they couldn't be pleased and

126

Tropical Melodrama

men were damned if they acted macho or sensitive.

Barbed wire, rusted and torn, never looked so good, as the barbed wire David saw beside Keala's truck, which indicated they had made it back. David made Becky a nest on the truck bench in the back and sat in front at her feet to hold her and keep her from bouncing too hard on the way back.

The ride was torturous, every rut hurt. It seemed like an eternity before they reached the highway at Kealia Beach. David stretched as Keala waited to go out onto the highway and into the beach parking area. Becky sat up and made a feeble attempt at putting her brown locks in some kind of order. Their mouths then dropped wide open as Keala blithely passed by the entrance to Kealia and tore up the highway toward his home.

They banged on the truck window with as much might as they could muster. Where was that maniac taking them now? Keala ignored their banging and they soon gave it up. The man was out of their control.

The truck clunked to a stop in its nesting spot in Keala's front yard, instantly becoming again the picture of an old wreck, which had sat idle for years. David helped Becky up, then turned on Keala.

"Hey, man, we expected you to drop us at Kealia Beach where our rental car is. What's the story?"

"Ah, brah, I can no let you go lik dat," Keala said. "We been tru' a lot toget'er. We gotta talk story, share

127

Kauai Calling

a little beer, chow down, mebbe a little music, den you go. You an the missus wash up. I fire up the barbecue. Cook dat Kala fish. 'Don worry, be happy, lik da man say. We have good time."

What choice did they have? They certainly were in no shape to walk back to Kealia. Becky accepted a mu'u mu'u from Lorna and went into the bathroom to soak in the tiny tub. Every part of her body stung as she lowered herself into the hot water. But once the stinging stopped she realized she was feeling quite happy, a trilly, zingy kind of happiness. She hummed to herself.

A knock on the door. "Hey, can I come in," David called.

"Sure," she said, standing up, reaching over and unlocking the door. "I'm about ready for someone to dry my back."

"How you feeling?" he asked as he came in and quickly shut the door behind him.

"A bit battered and bruised, but okay. Actually more than okay. Maybe it was the brush with death, but I'm feeling ridiculously happy."

"I heard you singing. Dinner's almost ready." His brown eyes were soft and moist as he gazed at her through the steam from her bath. "God, you look so good to me. That was awful," he said. "When I came down that chute looking for you and couldn't find you in that whirlpool, I thought you had drowned. You must have gotten free just as I went in."

"Maybe you bounced me out," Becky said. "My hero."

"Keala's the hero. By the way, you didn't look too unhappy cradled in his arms on the way back."

Becky started to protest his assumption, then a sparkle lit her brown eyes. "I wasn't."

"Unhappy?"

"Right. I enjoyed it. Felt like Jane to his Tarzan of the Jungle."

"See, Jerry's right. You women say you want warm, sensitive men, then get turned on by a caveman."

"I don't think it would wear well, though," she whispered. "It might be hard to discuss The Sunday New York Times with Tarzan. I wonder if he's pure Hawaiian. Do Hawaiians have curly hair like his?"

"He says he's about twenty ethnic groups including Caucasian, Samoan, Chinese, Portuguese, everything, including Hawaiian. He and I were just talking about that Kahuna in Kokee and your sign from the fish.

He told me that a Kahuna from the island of Maui sits right now at the base of Anahola Mountain trying to call back people he calls the Rainbow people, who were scattered when the islands split apart from a great cataclysm, like an ocean earthquake, thousands of years ago. Says those rainbow people were reincarnated into every nation on earth and are being summoned to Kauai. Maybe, he says, you're one of them and that's why you got that idea staring at the

Tropical Melodrama

129

Kauai Calling

mountain. Pretty weird, huh?"

"I'm not so sure it is weird. Maybe that's what happened," Becky said. "I've felt drawn here ever since I read about Kauai and I was staring at Anahola Mountain when I got that sudden urge to move."

"Please," David said, irritated in spite of himself.

"David, just consider it," Becky said, annoyed.

"You still want to move here after today?" David asked.

"I think so," Becky answered, smiling at him, then getting out of the tub.

"Hey, you two, suppa,'" Keala called.

While Becky toweled off and put on Lorna's mu'u mu'u that barely covered her calves, David jumped into the tub to wash his wounds. There were no clean clothes for him to put on. Keala weighed at least twice as much he did, but at least his bloody, torn and dirty ones wouldn't feel so bad if he were clean.

Supper was served outside in the open garage where three picnic tables crowded the space instead of a car. They were surprised to find at least a half dozen people had gathered there. All of them anxious to hear a retelling of their story and rescue from slippery slide. Their unicorn fish, wrapped in banana leaves, sat in the center of a huge platter surrounded by purple sweet potatoes interspersed with bright yellow mangoes. Smelling it, hunger grabbed David like a hook.

Later, in the twilight after supper, ukeleles, guitars and an old gut bucket appeared and the music began.

"'Dis 'da way we used to be on Kauai before 'da crazy cable television wreck our island life. We sit every night and sing," the old lady, who played the gut bucket, told Becky.

It was almost midnight before they could persuade Keala to leave his party long enough to drive them to their car, which they prayed was still there and in one piece at Kealia Beach. At first they didn't spot it as they came down the hill because a bunch of local people were sitting on its hood drinking beer under the full moon.

Before leaving them, Keala insisted on regaling the car sitters with the story of their misadventure at Slippery Slide and the beautiful Kala, or Unicorn fish that had given itself to Becky. After their story had been shared and digested and they had listened to at least one account from each participant about a rescue or a magical event that happened to that person or a relative, they said their goodbyes and thanked Keala and the crowd.

Keala kissed Becky on the lips and told her that from now on he would always be responsible for her, since he had saved her, and that he would take that responsibility very seriously. "I call you tomorrow at the Hyatt," he said, "and you give me your numba' back home."

Becky and David headed back to the hotel feeling weary, but delighted. Now that they were safe and on

131

Kauai Calling

their way they were pleased to have shared such a purely island kind of day.

"Oh man, I feel like I've been living in some old fashioned tropical melodrama," David said. "I don't think I could handle that much excitement and company on a day to day basis."

"But honestly, David, doesn't it make life back home seem dull?" Becky asked. "When is the last time you remember us being with that many people in an informal gathering like that? And tonight we were part of two of them. It is a shame that TV and the Internet have made all of us on the mainland so isolated from each other. That was fun sitting around swapping stories and singing old songs and sharing food. And wasn't that dinner absolutely delicious? Best fish I've ever tasted. Even just now telling those surfers at Kealia about our Slippery Slide adventure I had a blast."

"'Talking story', they call it," David said. "Only one thing bothers me about today. I'm not sure I like the idea of Keala taking responsibility for your life from now on."

"Hmm, two men to lean on. Not bad."

"Didn't take you long to lose your feminism."

"Hey, why not have both."

"Still want to move to Kauai?" David asked.

"Nothing that happened today changed my mind, though I'm sure I'll never go down the Slippery Slide again. What are you thinking about it?"

"Well, I guess I might as well tell you," David

said. "When I was searching for you in that whirlpool I swore I would live anywhere you wanted if God would only give you back to me."

"You prayed, David?"

"Yeah."

"So since I survived, you'll move here?" she asked her voice hopeful.

"If that's what you are sure that you want."

"Well, I would want you to want it too."

"That will be more a bit more difficult. I'd do it for you out of gratitude, but I can't make myself want to live so far from the action."

"What action?" Becky asked impatiently. "What do you mean when you say action?"

"Tomorrow, Becky," David said. "Tonight, I'm much too weary."

Kauai Calling

Chapter Five

She Knows You

Morning brought no new clarity to their dispute. Becky knew that if they stayed on opposite sides of this fence she would lose because she would not move to Kauai without him. She wondered why she had continued to push the point, when it only served to solidify David's stance.

"Let's give it a rest," she said over breakfast.

"Fine with me," he said. "My body feels as if I was run over by a truck. I don't need to be emotionally slammed, too."

"I'm sorry, 'Sweetie'," she replied while stroking his brown locks tenderly. "Today we'll recuperate. I'm just as beat. Let's get a massage and lie in the sun."

"Good plan. What were we going to do today?"

Kauai Calling

"I thought we might catch a whale watch sometime today and I really want to check out a Hawaiian healer who is giving a seminar at the Koloa library," Becky said. "This lady is called a Kahuna, too. I didn't think you would want to go."

"What time?"

"Three o'clock."

"Let's see how we're feeling by then. I might go," David said. "Maybe she could explain why I keep hearing that old guy, since she's also a Kahuna. Or maybe I'll check out the whale watch while you're there. Right now I just want to lie in the sun and heal."

By two o'clock that day, after alternately soaking in the sun and the Jacuzzi and a long massage after lunch, they were feeling a bit more energetic and decided to see if they could do both the lecture at the library and the whale watch out of Kukui'ula Harbor.

At the library they found a large crowd had arrived to hear Aunty Margaret. Since it was too large of a crowd for indoors, they decided to gather outside under the trees. A portly Hawaiian woman with dark eyes, wide lips that framed a friendly broad smile, and long, white hair, stood serenely under a red, furry blossomed Lehua Tree waiting for people to get settled. Beach mats and low beach chairs were sprinkled across the grass. As soon as Aunty Margaret spoke the crowd hushed.

She lectured about healing herbs and the benefits of sea salt and soaking in the ocean, then talked of

She Knows You

Kauai as the separate kingdom and the healing place where all Hawaiians travel to renew themselves. She told them that she was from the Big Island and had come to Kauai for spiritual renewal. After her short lecture she invited questions from the audience. Many of those who questioned her were invited to come forward so she could touch them or examine their skin and eyes.

The healer's quiet conviction, wide knowledge and ability to hear others' point of view even convinced David that she had some kind of uncommon power. Those in the audience who knew her treated her with the deference given royalty.

Becky urged David to ask her about the Kahuna in Koke'e and the chanting, but he wasn't about to bring up that painful subject in front of all of these people. Becky offered to ask for him, but he looked horrified and she knew better than to embarrass him that way.

David, though very interested, still wanted to make sure they got to the whale watch on time. He was about to suggest leaving when during the question and answer period, the chanting voice again rang in his head and he knew he had to try to find out about it, even if, as he hoped, this voice would disappear when they left the island.

After the formal program ended and the audience had applauded enthusiastically, David went forward and stood to the side waiting for a chance to ask his question privately. Many other participants also gathered around Aunty Margaret, eagerly straining to catch every word she spoke. There were so many waiting, David was sure they would miss their whale watch if they stayed. He looked at Becky and pointed to his watch. But she waved away his concern. "David, this is more important," she whispered. Two women in front of them trying to hear Aunty Margaret's words turned at once and shushed them.

David hated being shushed almost as much as he disliked new-age types, in which category he placed the two in front of him. He took Becky's arm and turned to go just as Aunty Margaret suddenly walked through the crowd and approached them.

When she reached him Aunty Margaret took his hand, looked deeply into his brown eyes and said very firmly, "You must listen, my son. Not with this." She pointed to his head. "But with this." She touched his heart. "Your heart is calling you."

That was all. She was gone before he could ask a question. Some of those who had been waiting looked at him annoyed that he had gotten her attention when they hadn't. Others seemed awestruck that Aunty Margaret had chosen him, as if her magic could have rubbed off on him. It reminded him a bit of the way people reacted to the Dalai Lama.

Listen to what? David wondered. What did it mean his heart was calling him? She had told him nothing. Just more mumbo jumbo he didn't understand.

She Knows You

He would have dismissed the whole encounter, except goose bumps rose on his arms. A local woman rubbed his skin and said, "Ooh, chicken skin. She give you chicken skin."

"Let's get out of here," he said to Becky and walked away briskly toward the car.

"David, wait," Becky said, feeling as if she must apologize to the local woman and those others he'd turned away from so rudely. She gave them a wan, apologetic smile and followed him to the car.

"You could have at least acted as if you appreciated her attention when other people were waiting, instead of being so brusque," she said when she reached him. "We're guests here. She did you a favor choosing you."

"What favor?" David asked. "I didn't get to ask her a question. 'Listen to my heart.' Whoopie! Sounds like a song from some sentimental musical."

"Well, I thought she was definitely impressive," Becky said. "I think she was trying to tell you to use your feelings more and your head less. That makes sense to me and I know you."

"But what does that have to do with continually hearing chanting in my head?" David demanded as he started the car.

"I don't know, but I do know she singled you out for attention so I think it meant something."

"All those psychic types talk cryptically so that whatever they say can be interpreted hundreds of ways

139

Kauai Calling

No matter what happens to me in the future, I know that you, and probably Kat, will say, 'See David, that's what Aunty Margaret meant when she said, 'Listen to your heart.'"

David found an opening in the strolling crowd to back out the car and screeched the tires a little as he plowed through it. Becky cringed when she saw people nearby shaking their heads and frowning at him. She also made a mental note not to remind him of Aunty Margaret's comment or even to tell Kat about it.

They reached Kukuiula harbor, on the south shore, minutes later, just barely catching the last whale watch trip of the day, which according to their captain promised to be a good one. He said that whales, like fish, were more active at sunrise and sunset.

Dave, one of the crew, obligingly helped them aboard The 'Spirit of Kauai', a spacious state-of-the-art catamaran best suited he said, to traverse these Hawaiian waters.

"This is quite some boat!" David said to another crew member.

"Take a look inside the cabin, all teak lined." the crewman said.

After a quick tour around the vessel, Becky and David chose to sit out on the front trampoline-like area despite their wounds, to catch the breeze and be the first to see any whales that appeared. There were about 15 other couples aboard, all showing excited

She Knows You

anticipation. After a quick briefing and introduction to the staff by Captain Andy, they sailed out of the harbor at four o'clock on the dot. The first pod they spotted performed as if they were in a sea life park; spouting, fluke slapping, and even breaching in mighty thumps. Their activity excited other pods and soon there were whales all about them.

In the beginning of their trip David timed them and asked questions of Dave and Trent, the crew members, but after a few pokes from Becky, he dispensed with his intellectual questioning and just enjoyed watching them. He even forgot his adult dignity and shouted like an excited child each time he spotted a whale. Becky was amazed at the views of the island, the rich red dirt and green of the sugar cane created a most spectacular patchwork. It was also apparent where man had taken hold, but civilization appeared to only hug the coastline, it was like so much of the island seemed untamed from this view by sea. Sailing was clearly another way to enjoy Kauai from a different and unique perspective.

About halfway through their trip, an appetizing array of pupus from wings to fresh tropical fruits and cheeses were set out and "Sneaky Tikis" were served. David and Becky hadn't eaten in their haste to see the Kahuna and in the rush to get to the harbor, so David was one of the first in line to load up a plate for both of them. The entire crew milled about to make sure each guest felt welcome and satisfied. Dave approached

141

Kauai Calling

Becky and asked how she was enjoying the cruise.

"We are having a terrific time, I especially notice that there's a lot of the 'Aloha Spirit' here." Becky said.

"It's cuz, we all love being out on the water,"He replied.

"I don't think that anyone aboard wouldn't rate this as one of the best things they've done, it couldn't be more perfect," she added.

"Like Andy says, 'Nobody has more fun,'"Dave said with a warm smile as David returned to his seat, signaling for help from Becky, plate overflowing.

The second hour of their trip passed like minutes. No one could believe it when Andy announced it was time to go back to shore. They were heading in when a whale surfaced and swam toward them. The captain cut his engine and they drifted quietly on the water as the whale steadily approached. The law prohibited the boat from coming within 300 feet of a whale, but no one could stop a whale from coming by the boat.

"We're here until that baby moves," Dave said.

No one on board complained. David's jaw went slack as the whale came alongside their boat on the starboard side.

"Most likely she's female and there are a couple of males after her. She's using us to discourage them," Trent said. "This time of year they mate before they go back to Alaska. She's probably already pregnant."

"'Tiny', look, she's looking right at me," David

She Knows You

said, as the whale turned slightly. Becky noticed the whale's eye did seem to be focused on him and her fin waved as she stared at them.

"It looks like she knows you," Becky teased.

"Can I reach over the side and touch her?" David asked the captain, without shifting his gaze from the whale.

"Sure, if she'll let you." David reached out and touched the leathery gray skin of the humpback who stretched out longer than the entire side of the catamaran. "Just be careful. If that baby wants to knock us over, she easily can," Andy said.

Even though David could no longer reach the whale, his hand was still stretched over the side of the boat and he looked dazed. The head of the humpback did not resemble the giant square head of Gepetto's whale, and the body though huge, did not look as if it could contain the little room he had imagined himself in as a child, but none of that mattered. Just being so close to a whale made his heart flutter. In his excitement devoid of even a tinge of irony or skepticism he truly felt like a boy again.

"Look, everyone," Captain Andy shouted. "See, those two whales over there." He pointed at two enormous whales that had risen to the surface and were slapping their flukes. They are the problem, I'll bet. We think that fluke slapping is sexual display behavior to impress this one by the rail. But she likes us better."

They witnessed a technicolor sunset at sea, and

Kauai Calling

as darkness fell, they were finally able to safely turn on the engine and sail back to shore. Everyone on board chattered excitedly all the way in. The experience had turned strangers into friends. Even the boat's crew were brimming with excitement. When they reached shore Captain Andy bought some fish from a fishing boat in the harbor and invited anyone who would like to stay and join in a fish fry celebration.

"Sure wish that would happen every day," the captain said to Becky and David, as the charcoal warmed on the grill.

"Me, too," David said. "Maybe we'll go with you tomorrow instead of to the North shore."

"Have you seen the North Shore yet?" Andy asked.

"Nope, and tomorrow's our last day. We've seen some amazing and exciting things here, but nothing to match that whale coming alongside the boat."

The captain shook his head. "Don't miss the North Shore, man. It's the most beautiful place on earth. Hanalei Bay. The Na Pali Coast. Lumahai Beach. Naw, don't go out with us again on your last day, go to the North Shore. You won't regret it.

Chapter Six

A Different World

On their last full day on Kauai, David and Becky were determined to cover as much of the North Shore as possible. They barely glanced at Kealia Beach as they passed by, though Becky felt a chill as the road traveled over the Kealia River. Her body might have floated out through the mouth of that river into the ocean if Keala hadn't saved her.

At Anahola she stared inland at the mountain with its fascinating, irregular, King Kong-like summit and wondered if that Kahuna Keala had mentioned was still sitting there. It did seem as if her desire to live on Kauai was heightened by looking at that particular mountain. She mentioned it to David as he zipped past.

Kauai Calling

"Power of suggestion, maybe," he said, "though I gotta admit I have had some strange experiences here that make the Kahuna calling the rainbow people back sound almost plausible."

"Besides the chanting you hear?" Becky asked.

"Yep."

"Like what?"

He looked at her, then back at the road. She knew he was deciding whether to confide in her. She liked this new softer, less absolute David. He seemed more open to other possibilities than she had ever known him to be. But she also guessed it made him feel vulnerable and uncomfortable.

"Well, I'm not sure it isn't just coincidence, but . . . well, when we were out on that whale watch . . ."

"What about it?" she asked, turning her body to face him as he drove.

"Phew. Don't laugh."

"I'm not laughing. Tell me."

"Okay. Now, you promised, no laughing. Well, yesterday, each time I asked to see whales, within seconds, we saw them. Honest." He glanced at her to see how she was reacting. His eyes back on the road, he added, "You know that whale that came alongside the boat?"

"What about it?"

"I asked to be able to touch one, then it came."

"Really?"

"Yes, really," he said, smiling in spite of himself.

A Different World

"So now I'm not only hearing voices, I'm ordering natural phenomena about."

"Psycho-pomps," Becky said.

"Maybe. Whatever is going on, it is shaking up my predictable world. Big time."

"Does that upset you," Becky asked.

"Upset is not the word. It's unsettling. It's destroying my world order. If one of us was going to have this kind of unexplainable experience, I would expect it to happen to you, not me."

"I can't even picture how I'll tell Jerry about what happened to me here," he said, shrugging his shoulders. "Now Kat that's another story. She'll love it."

When the island circled past Kilauea, they detoured to the lighthouse and bird sanctuary, their first north shore destination. On the promontory of the lighthouse, high over the sea, they examined the blue footed boobies in their nests and watched the graceful, split tailed, Iwi birds circling through the air. Spinner dolphins cavorted in the water below the lighthouse, as if performing for the visitors above them.

"Best spot on the island to see dolphins," the park ranger informed David. "Used to be able to go down there to Secret Beach and swim with them to your heart's content. Now it's against the law."

"Against the law?" David asked. "Why? Are they endangered?"

"Too many people harassing them. It changes their patterns," the ranger said. "No one is allowed

147

Kauai Calling

closer than 300 feet."

David felt his disappointment keenly. His other fantasy of Kauai, beside watching whales spout and breach, had been to swim with the dolphins, or at least see them up close in the water. After the park ranger walked away, Becky said, "If we lived here I bet you could find a spot to swim with them."

"I thought that subject was closed."

"It's barely been opened," she said.

"You know what, Becky." Suddenly his voice had that cold, formal sound she hated. "I'd like to enjoy this last day without getting pestered about moving to Kauai. Even if I would consider it, I couldn't decide in two days and you know it."

Yeah, she did know it. A slow-moving freight train didn't stop or turn quickly. "Sorry," she said. "You're right. We'll drop it for now. I won't bring it up again today. We'll talk about it when we get home."

He nodded and smiled a soft, wry grin. "Great. Thanks. Let's hit all the 'must see' spots on the north shore. Snorkel at the end of the road. Maybe take a hike up the first part of the Na Pali. That suit you?"

"Except for the snorkeling. Today I'll just beach it."

As they made their way around the north shore, they visited Hanalei and Lumahai Beach, and the wet cave at Haena. The surf was up at each spot. They enjoyed watching the high rollers come in and crash high on the beach. But, except for a few brave surfers,

A Different World

no one was swimming at any of the spots where they stopped.

At Ke'e Beach Park, at the end of the road, they found fewer tourists than they had expected on the beach, because quite a bit of it was wet from the high surf. Ke'e lagoon, almost enclosed by lava rock, like Lydgate, had a wide exit at the west end, which allowed access to the ocean. Their guide book had promised this to be a safe, comfortable snorkeling spot. But today the waves crashed over the lava walls and churned the water, making it murky. No one snorkeled in the water. The red life guard stand stood empty as the surf was too rough for swimming or snorkeling.

"Darn," David said, surveying the foaming water from the beach.

"You're not going in there, I hope," Becky said. "That sign says the lagoon is dangerous when the red flag is flying. There's the red flag." She pointed at it in the middle of the beach. The sand around it wet and foamy.

"I'm not staying out of the ocean on my last day," David said, studying the roiling waters. "It doesn't look too bad over there toward the east end away from the outlet to the ocean. I'll give it a try. You don't mind, do you?" he asked Becky.

"Just be careful, David," she said. "After yesterday, believe me, I know unknown waters can be treacherous."

"Hey, look on the bright side. If I drown, 'Tiny',

149

Kauai Calling

you can move to Kauai with no hassles. Keala will watch over you and help you spend my insurance, too," he quipped.

"Hmm, maybe if Keala weren't married . . ."

"I think you'd get sick of Keala real quick from the banal conversation I overheard between him and Lorna." Then he smiled at her. "But I'm glad you'd like to keep me, even though I am a stodgy, old, pain in the butt."

"Hmm, maybe I should think that over again," she answered, spreading her beach mat and towel over the large, flat, brown leaves that dotted the sand on the beach.

"You do that. I'll snorkel."

"I'll see if I can find a nice place for a late lunch. I'm in the mood for a place like Peter Luger." she said, checking the sun angle before settling down on her towel to read the guide book.

David adjusted his snorkel and mask, but decided to leave his fins behind because they were so awkward and the lagoon offered little opportunity to swim far. Murky water colored by the red dirt and the churning of sand afforded him few opportunities to observe the fish along the east side and so he ventured out to the far wall. There he found a large parrot fish and some yellow and black angel fish, whose brilliant colors shone through the murky water. Contented, he followed the parrot fish as it nibbled its way along the rocky wall. His ears enclosed by water only

A Different World

occasionally picked up the crash of a wave over the wall.

As he swam along after the fish, he thought about what it might be like to live on this island. On the one hand the land area was small and he feared he'd get what one man had referred to as "rock fever," on the other, the enclosing sea was vast and spread all around them. What attracted him most to Kauai was the sea and its inhabitants.

An eel poked its lizard-like head out of an opening in a rock and shocked the parrot fish. It darted quickly away, David in hot pursuit. He lost sight of the fish in the clouds of churning water and raised his head to check on his whereabouts. Just as he realized he was in the channel to the ocean, a huge wave caught him up and swept him toward the beach, his brown hair now covering his line of sight. Before he could recover his balance and right himself, it had crashed against the incline of the beach, then grabbed him up again and was sweeping him back out through the channel.

Panic flooded him, every pore in his body seemed to be screaming in terror. The Kahuna's loud chants suddenly rang in his ears. The large wave had happened so quickly, he was sure no one had seen him go. He forced himself to calm down, knowing panic would rob him of breath and drown him.

He finally was able to push his head above water, tore off his mask and searched for the shore. The last time he had looked for Becky, while still in the

151

Kauai Calling

lagoon, she had her head buried in the guide book and few other people were on the beach.

The high rolling waves were coming thick and fast now. When at last he spotted the beach, it looked like a tiny spit of land. To the west he could see the magnificent outline of the Na Pali cliffs far down the coast. Waves he might have enjoyed floating over if he were close to shore, he now knew as his enemy. He yelled a few times when he could keep his head above water, but there was no point. Who could possibly hear or even see him over the crashing swells? His only hope was that Becky would notice he was missing. But what if she thought he'd just wandered off to explore the heiau area or the start of the Na Pali?

I don't believe this is happening, he thought. He should have asked Becky to keep an eye on him. Instead he had teased her about worrying.

He looked out to sea and saw an enormous wave coming toward him. Thank God, those waves weren't breaking at this spot, he thought, or he'd broken in two. How he wished he'd worn his fins. They might have given him a fighting chance.

He made himself stop struggling with the water and roll on his back and float up the wave's face while he thought through what his options were. He could not fight for control of this situation; if he did, he would be lost, even though it was his usual way to gain dominance. But how could his puny little self gain control over the mighty Pacific Ocean?

A Different World

As he floated, he thought of Becky discovering him gone. He didn't appreciate Becky enough. Hadn't told her how much he enjoyed the life she brought to him. Keala said she was magical and the man was right, she was magical. He wished her intuition would jar her right now, and she would sense him in danger and send help.

All he could see along the shore at the wave crests was rocky coast. From this distance out in the sea he could not even spot a speck of sand. Even if he could swim to shore, he would be dashed against the sharp lava rocks by the waves and killed.

Fighting to stay afloat, he felt tired and sad. He hadn't yet lived the life he wanted to live. He'd sacrificed the moment to prepare for that life and now the end was definitely looming. Once again he heard the old Kahuna chanting and suddenly, as if by magic, he understood his chant as a warning about this very moment. He even understood why that Kahuna had called him Jonah.

"Hey, Jonah." That's what the old Kahuna had said. "Hey, Jonah." He searched his memory trying to bring back the rest of the phrase. "Beeg hou," the van driver had said meant "big trouble." And then there was something about "one water." Maybe this water, the Pacific Ocean. Nah, his head rejected his conjectures. But something deeper in him, maybe his heart said, "Yes," and he was convinced that it was right.

153

Kauai Calling

At the apex of the next wave he realized he was moving eastward away from the lagoon and further out to sea. He realized that he must be caught in a riptide, because even when he swam against it, he continued to be carried out on it. He remembered learning during life saving lessons that the only way to deal with a rip tide is to swim diagonally out of it.

Just then a massive wave swept him up and he saw he was being carried shoreward fast. The island loomed up in front of him, but then he realized if this wave crashed with him up on it, it would break him in pieces. He swam desperately off the top of the wave and didn't breathe again until he lay in the trough between it and the next one. Just as he had convinced himself to relax and flow with the water, hoping a helicopter or boat might spot him, something big bumped his leg.

Sharks! He fought to stem the panic tightening his muscles again. Down next to his thigh, he saw a large silver object. God, it was a shark. Bile rose in his throat. His heart thumped louder than the surf crashing. The thing raised itself and he saw its face.

Not a shark. A short stubby face and a glittering black eye. A dolphin. Not a shark. A dolphin. The joy he experienced rivaled any he had ever felt in his life; like the basket he shot that won the big game, or that bike he got the Christmas his dad was out of work.

He treaded water and whispered, "Help me. Please help me." Had he ever asked for help so directly

A Different World

before, he wondered.

The dolphin seemed to understand or else it was just curious because it swam closer and inspected him with the same fervor he gave it. David reached out his hand and touched its silver flesh gingerly. When he pulled his hand back, the dolphin nudged his chest with its nose. David's panic subsided, though not sure why, he trusted this creature that was looking at him. The dolphin squeaked, then nudged his shoulder. It knocked him off balance and he swallowed some water. As he choked it back up, the dolphin raised him by putting its head under David's chest. When he stopped coughing and could rest on the dolphin, David wondered if this intelligent sea creature could get him to shore? Save him? He had heard stories of such rescues by dolphins but had never really taken them seriously. The dolphin moved out from below him as if reading his thoughts and came up beside him and again nudged him toward the shore. David, with joy in his heart and newfound energy in his arms, stroked in a mighty crawl toward the coast, though he still wondered how he would get ashore in the crashing waves.

While David snorkeled, Becky had finished her reading and drifted off to sleep on the beach. She awoke with a startle and immediately knew something was wrong. She searched for David in the shallower parts of the water, but couldn't find him. She ran up the long path to the heiau, but saw only a few tourists

Kauai Calling

on the rocky climb. She asked everyone she met if they had seen him.

"Probably using the john," one man offered.

"Could you check the men's restrooms for me?" she begged.

"Please, hurry, he was snorkeling. I fell asleep and now I can't find him," Becky explained.

"Not too bright on a day like this. What about his gear? Anything on the shore?" the man asked.

Becky ran back to check until she could see the beach where only their towels and backpack lay. None of David's snorkeling gear was around. She looked back at the man and shook her head sadly. By now she was choking back her tears. The man sauntered over to the rest rooms, Becky running ahead of him, pleaded, "Please, hurry."

"Lady, if your buddy is out in that surf, my hurrying ain't gonna help, and if he's in the restroom it won't matter." But he did speed up a little and came out shaking his head, then shrugged.

Becky ran back to their beach mats, praying David had brought his cell phone, even though she had made him promise not to carry it when they went out. She dumped the contents of his backpack out on the beach towel and it wasn't there. She burst into tears.

At that moment a shy, blonde boy about fourteen came over to her and said, "Hi, my name's Jesse and I heard you a little while ago say your friend's lost out in the ocean. Is that right?"

It took a moment to comprehend what he said. "Yes. Yes," she said distractedly, when his words got through to her.

"I was watching him . . ."

"Oh, thank God . . ."

". . . I was trying to decide if it was okay to swim or not and I saw him go out the channel on a wave."

"Oh no," she cried, "out the channel?"

"Yeah," Jesse said, "and I didn't see him come back, either."

"Oh my God! I've got to find a phone. Do you know where I can find a phone?" Becky exclaimed.

"I got one," the boy said. "My mom's a worrywart. She makes me carry it when I go hiking or to the beach."

Becky ran with the boy to his towel and took the little cell phone he offered and called 911.

The dispatcher asked what seemed like endless stupid questions while Becky wanted to scream at her, 'just find him'. But she was too polite to scream, even in that moment of panic. The dispatcher promised to radio all the boats out in the water, although she said there are probably not many because of the high surf. She also told Becky that they'd send the ocean rescue boat and ask the tour helicopters to search the area.

"Meanwhile," the dispatcher said in a kind voice, "you search that area thoroughly. Most times people have just come in at a different spot or wandered off on a little expedition. Just below the park there's a

Kauai Calling

secluded strip of beach where a lot of folks sunbathe nude, so look down there because men like to wander down when their mate isn't looking. Maybe that's where you'll find him."

Jesse gave the dispatcher the number of the cell phone, before Becky hung up. She ran down the beach in the direction the dispatcher had suggested. Jesse ran with her until he saw a few naked people, then he turned red and backed away.

Becky, too, felt shy walking up to the sunbathing nudes, but her fear overcame her reticence and she asked each one she came upon if they had seen David strolling down the beach. One man, who made no attempt to cover his manliness assured her that someone in a swimsuit would be quite noticeable, since sunbathing nude, though tolerated on this beach, was not actually legal. Any clothed male would be suspect as possibly a cop.

Far out from the spot where Becky questioned the sunbather, David swam with the dolphin close by his side. He'd been pushing hard and had started to tire. Every time his panic escalated in him he looked at the dolphin and felt reassured.

Then the dolphin abruptly dove down deep and David was afraid that it had left him. Seconds later, he heard a splash in front of him and saw another dolphin arc through the water in a synchronized leap with his dolphin companion. The two dolphins dove down and David saw their glossy, silver bodies pass beneath him.

A Different World

In the blink of an eye they reappeared back at the surface, one on either side of him.

Though his condition remained precarious, even with the dolphins beside him, elation filled and buoyed him like a balloon filling with helium. He extended his arms and touched the sides of each dolphin and found that he could rest his arms that way and they would pull him along with them. With their support he felt almost as seaworthy as a dolphin. Maybe, as Kat would say, he was one in a former life.

He wondered if Becky was looking for him yet, and wished if he was going to perish, she could know how magical these last moments had been for him. If only she could see him swimming with the dolphins. "David and the Magic Dolphins," sounded like a Disney film.

In a moment of stillness, between waves, he heard the rumbling sound of an engine. Though he tried, he could see nothing over the tall swells. The dolphins moved in closer on each side of him, and as if reading his thoughts pushed him up, leaning his arms on their backs. He then spotted a large black rubber raft, like the kind tourists ride to the Na Pali Coast. Amazed at the amount of noise the raft engine made, he looked up in the sky and saw a helicopter hovering overhead.

He waved his arms and shouted, then realized the helicopter had already spotted him and was guiding the raft to him. A blazing flare dropped down beside

Kauai Calling

him.

    The dolphins suddenly dove down and he was left alone treading water. His relief at being found was tempered slightly by his sorrow at losing his dolphins. The boat moved toward him slowly. He was still not sure they could see him.

    With a mighty splash and a high arc above the water the dolphins shot up into the air, dove down, came up again spinning on their tails in perfect unison. Abruptly, they circled round and swam back, taking up their escort duty on either side of him. The men in the boat, following the dolphins' trajectory, yelled and pointed to him. David waved to the boaters, then tried to hug his dolphin saviors.

    The boat pilot pulled the raft as close as he could and threw a life preserver to David. A crew member dove overboard with a life jacket and swam toward him. David giggled. Relief at his rescue? The joy of swimming with the dolphins? He was not sure why, but laughter just bubbled up and spilled out of him as his human rescuer swam toward him.

    When the man reached within feet of David, the dolphins sped up and swam away. As David was helped into the life jacket, the helicopter overhead swooped up and away. Tugging on the line, the boat crewman helped David swim to the raft where many hands grabbed him at once, pulling him up and over the side.

    Once he was safely aboard, the two dolphins

A Different World

again arced their bodies in front of the boat, spun on their tails as if taking a final bow and were gone. Even the most hard bitten sea rescue crewmen cheered at the dramatic display. David watched transfixed, oblivious to the tears flowing down his cheeks.

The captain radioed back to shore that they had David safely aboard and added, "Hey brah, you ain' neva gonna believe dis dude's story. I hardly believe it, an I seen it with my own eyes."

Becky stood on a high spot of Ke'e Beach helplessly searching the water. In that moment she didn't care where she lived the rest of her life as long as she lived it with David. She realized now David was the home she'd searched for all her life, not the island. It was David's full concentrated presence here on vacation with her, plus the island's beauty, that had made this place seem like the long sought after "home" she'd always wanted.

The surf subsided and she could see great stretches through the binoculars Jesse had also lent her. In the distance she heard the whir of a helicopter and prayed that they had spotted him.

A police siren screamed. Becky ran back toward the parking lot and saw the police car coming, its blue lights flashing. Jesse and his mother, who had come for him a short time ago, joined her.

The police car screeched to a halt and an officer jumped out just as Becky reached the big boulders separating the beach from the road. Her knees felt

Kauai Calling

weak and for just an instant she didn't want to know, wanted time to prepare herself for the news if it were bad. Jesse's mom put her arms around Becky's shoulders and braced her. Jesse hovered protectively on her other side.

"We got 'im," the policeman yelled as he jumped out of his car in front of her. "We got him. They're bringing him into Tunnels Beach right now. I came to get you."

"He's okay?"

"They said he's fine. 'Said dolphins rescued him. We gotta go, so we can be there when he gets in."

Becky hugged Jesse and thanked him and his mom for waiting with her and helping her, then jumped in the police car. With sirens wailing they sped out of the park.

At Tunnel's, Becky ran ahead, but then didn't know what path to take. She let the policeman pass her, then followed close behind. His radio crackled and he answered.

"We're almost in," a male voice shouted. "Got his lady with me," the policeman replied. "Ma'am, that's them coming in right now." He pointed to a black raft pulling up toward the far end of the beach. Becky sprinted down the soft sand after the officer. Her feet had never flown so fast or her body felt so light. He was safe. She could see him. As she ran she cried in great gulping sobs.

The crewmen from the boat were helping David

A Different World

ashore when he spotted her. He broke from them and tried to run toward her. A twinge pierced his side, doubling him over, but it didn't matter. He straightened up just in time for her to fly into his arms. The circle of people around the two of them wore faces wreathed in broad grins. Soon a babble of voices arose as each told his or her version of the story.

"Dolphins?" Becky asked when she finally could catch her breath.

"Dolphins," David said. "I got to swim with the dolphins, for real."

"You must have been terrified," Becky said.

"Not after the dolphins came. I almost wished my rescue had come later."

"What?" Becky yelped.

"Just teasing," David said with a tired grin. "I was very happy to see that boat and the helicopter, but it was a special time swimming with those dolphins."

The patrolman who had brought Becky insisted on taking them back right away to Ke'e Beach Park, because he had to go back to work. They thanked David's rescuers, who dismissed their part in the rescue as all in a day's work.

Back at Ke'e Beach a small group waited to hear the end of the story. After satisfying them with the details, Becky introduced David to Jesse and his mother, Carla. David thanked Jesse for his help and wanted to reward him with some money.

But the boy shyly refused it, saying, "Nah, that's

163

Kauai Calling

okay. I like helping people."

"And thank you, ma'am for making him carry a cell phone," David said to his mother.

"Amen," Becky added, knowing why David had emphasized the words.

After the others left, Becky and David put their beach things in the car and decided to climb up to Laka's platform in the ancient heiau to watch the sunset and to offer thanks to the dolphins, and the keeper of this island for David's rescue.

They edged around the ocean on a muddy gravel strewn walkway until they came to a steep incline where they climbed up the side of the cliff. Half way up, a sign told them about this hula platform and heiau where the Goddess Laka danced. David felt the dog tiredness in his legs from all the exertion earlier, but it didn't deter him. Their narrow steep path was bordered on each side by stones and dirt until they stepped out onto a beautiful hilltop headland strewn with boulders and low grass. Above them stood the evenly piled stones of the heiau platform. Behind it a steep wall led up to the top of the Na Pali and the trail that led to Kalalau.

The Pacific stretched out into infinity before them on three sides. Below, to the East, Ke'e Beach looked like a postage stamp, its turquoise lagoon a kiddie pool. From this height the Pacific seemed as calm as its name proclaimed, though the sound of waves crashing against the cliffs below them clearly announced that the

A Different World

ocean was neither quiet, nor peaceful.

Becky and David sat arm in arm on the hillside below the heiau. For a long time they stared out to sea, each encapsulated in thoughts of gratitude and wonder about his rescue. Finally Becky broke the silence and asked, "David, what are you thinking?".

"I was wishing those two dolphins would come, and I could show them to you, and thank them. Two days ago I would have scoffed at such an idea, but after today it doesn't seem at all absurd."

"I have a feeling they know you're as grateful as I am," she said. "They communicate in ways that we just don't understand."

" Becky," he began tentatively. Saying this was hard for him but he wanted to say it. "I promise I will never laugh at that kind of stuff again. Dolphins as psycho-pomps? Cool. I believe it. I believe a lot of things I didn't believe this morning."

"You know what?" he continued. "While I was floating around out there, I heard exactly what that Kahuna said to me. I knew it as if he had spoken standard English. He said, 'Hey, Jonah, no go in that one water' meaning this ocean. Remember, how he pointed at the sea. He said, 'you no listen you in big hou, meaning, trouble.' It just came to me plain as day."

"But why would he call you 'Jonah?'" Becky asked. "Because he somehow knew you loved whales?"

"Nah," David said, shaking his head and tearing his gaze from the sea to look at Becky. "Remember, I

Kauai Calling

told you he reminded me of someone from my childhood? Well, our next door neighbor was a lady called Auntie Pualani. She was Hawaiian, maybe even came from Kauai. That's who he reminded me of, even looked a little like her, though she's probably dead by now."

"Are you saying that he was she in a past life?" Becky interrupted, excited by his story.

David frowned skeptically, then held up his hand. "Sorry, tell me the rest," she urged.

"Well, Auntie Pualani was my baby-sitter and she used to call me her little Jonah. She's the one that first told me the story of 'Jonah and the Whale' and read me Pinocchio. She told me lots of stories, but my favorites were always those two about living in the belly of a whale, so she nicknamed me 'Jonah'. Honestly, I forgot her until today."

"But how would the Kahuna know?" Becky asked.

"Now who is locked into rationalism?" David teased. "Becky, I don't know how to explain any of it. Why did you look at that mountain and insist we move here?"

"True," Becky said. "Kauai is magical. It's as if we entered a whole different world here. A world that doesn't in the least bit resemble New York."

"Yeah," David said. "It makes me feel a little woozy or off balance. Becky?" He waited until her brown eyes were fastened on his brown ones, then looked deeply into her eyes as if peering into her heart and soul. "Thank you for bringing me here to Kauai. Like Keala said, 'You are one magical lady'. You and this island have opened my mind, my heart and I guess my soul." He kissed her lips lightly. "I'll live here happily if that's what you want."

Becky took his face between her two hands and gently caressed his cheeks. How precious his face was to her. Her hands trembled as she thought of how close she'd come to losing him. Today, she'd found her old David, as well as, this new David. She'd found the man she'd thought she'd lost and more importantly a new, deeper David, a partner for her inner journey and a spiritually rich life.

"David," she said, "I know now that *you* are my home and any place I live with you, the way you are now, will be home to me."

They kissed, then turned and watched the sun set over the deepening blue of the sea. Not a cloud marred the sky. With their heads cradled together they discovered that now they shared the same horizon. As the last golden rays of the fiery sun dropped below the horizon, a brilliant green glow flashed.

The End

How much did you enjoy your book?
Send us an e-mail or quick note and we'll add
Your comments to our 'Reader's Reviews' page
at our Web-site:
www.ParadiseWorks-Inc.com

Do You have friends who would enjoy
starring in their very own romantic adventure
set here in Paradise- Kauai, Hawaii
where suspense, wonder, love and adventure
can surround them forever.
Let us bring them a very special gift
of a trip to Hawaii.

Paradise Works, Inc.
presents:

"Kauai Calling"

A romantic adventure set in a Hawaiian Paradise-Kauai. This professionally written and bound paperback book is an everlasting gift for any loved one.

Don't wait, order online today!
A Great Gift!
www.ParadiseWorks-Inc.com
E-mail: paradiseworks@hawaiian.net
1/808/742-2457
MasterCard/Visa accepted

Bringing You a "NOVEL" Piece of Paradise